"What kind of man are you?"

As she spoke, Caroline squirmed inwardly beneath his compelling gaze.

Gustav's hands closed on her shoulders. "I know what I want, and I'll stop at nothing to get it," he answered decisively.

"I'll feel sorry for you when you discover that money can't buy the one thing you'll want most—love!" Caroline retorted, struggling vainly to free herself.

"All I shall ever need is a woman in my bed from time to time, and women like that can always be bought."

"You're disgusting," Caroline cried. "Don't make me despise you more than I do already."

"You may despise me all you like," he laughed softly, pulling her closer. "You're beautiful when you're angry, my sweet wife, and it only makes me desire you more...."

YVONNE WHITTAL

the lion of la roche

Harlequin Books

TORONTO · LONDON · LOS ANGELES · AMSTERDAM
SYDNEY · HAMBURG · PARIS · STOCKHOLM · ATHENS · TOKYO

Harlequin Presents edition published April 1982
ISBN 0-373-10498-7

Original hardcover edition published in 1981
by Mills & Boon Limited

CHAPTER ONE

THE rain came down out of an ominous-looking sky as if the sluice gates of heaven had been opened, and the windscreen wipers of Caroline's small grey Austin were making a frantic, but totally ineffectual effort to ensure visibility. She had been travelling in this appalling weather for the past few hours since leaving Worcester behind her, and there was still no sign that the deluge might ease off. She should have reached the Lindsays' farm more than an hour ago, but instead she found herself driving along a seemingly endless, muddy road which apparently led to nowhere in particular.

To make matters worse, she finally had to admit to herself that she must have taken the wrong turning after leaving Matjiesfontein and, cursing herself for her stupidity, she swung the car about on the narrow road and went back the way she had come. The sky was darkening swiftly with approaching nightfall, and she realised that the only sensible thing to do would be to seek shelter for the night at a nearby farm from where she could telephone Dennis to inform him of her predicament. She grimaced now as she imagined his annoyance at her inability to follow the seemingly simple directions he had given her, but his annoyance was something she would just have to face.

Dennis Lindsay, her fiancé, was a stickler for punctuality, and also for doing the right time at the right time, and the right place. Some had labeled him self-righteous, while others had considered him a boring stick-in-the-mud, but Caroline had always found him dependable, and extremely honourable. These were two important qualities her father had never possessed in his lifetime, and it was, perhaps, for this reason that she admired Dennis so much. They had met, quite by chance, at the home of a mutual acquaintance two years ago and, as time passed, he had become her friend and adviser while he wooed her in that peculiar Victorian manner which was so misplaced in this modern, often promiscuous era they lived in. Two weeks ago, on the eve of his departure on a holiday to his parents' farm, he had taken her to dinner and had asked her to marry him, and she had agreed. This weekend at his home had been considered the appropriate time to inform his parents of their decision, and to make it officially known that they were engaged by placing that beautiful but elaborate diamond ring on her finger.

That was to have been this evening, Caroline sighed to herself as she manipulated the car round a sharp bend in the road, but the next moment her sigh was like a strangled cry of surprise in her throat as she put her foot down on the brake and brought the car to an abrupt, shuddering halt. Ahead of her, illuminated in the twin beams of the car's headlights, lay the low bridge she had crossed not more than an hour before, but it was now only barely visible beneath the swirling water that washed over it. Only a fool would take the chance of crossing it, she realised, and, pushing the gear lever into reverse, she released the clutch and accelerated. The rear end of the car seemed to lift with the effort, but the wheels spun senselessly, digging deeper into the mud. Caroline shifted gears in a panic, and tried again, but the Austin refused to shift an inch and, frustrated and tired, she lowered her head on to the steering wheel.

Nothing was going according to plan for her, and if weeping would have solved her problems at all at that moment, then she would have done so.

Desperate to reach her destination, she tried once more to ease her car out of the cloying mud, but it remained immovable as if the wheels had become glued to the soggy soil. Exasperated, she zipped up her thick woollen jersey and pushed her lanky fair hair into a matching cap before venturing out into the cold wet night. In the faltering light of her torch she saw that the wheels had dug far deeper into the mud than she had imagined, and she supposed dismally that it would be hours before someone found her on this deserted stretch of road. Despondent, and oblivious of the driving rain soaking slowly through her clothes, she extinguished her torch and leaned against the car for a moment while she tried to decide what to do for the best.

A light flickered through the trees several metres from the road, and her heart lifted hopefully. Perhaps there was someone, after all, who could help her out of this predicament she had landed herself in, she decided, and locking the doors of the Austin she strode determinedly towards the fence. She climbed through it, taking care not to tear her slacks on the nasty barbs and, saving her torch light as much as possible, she trudged up the slight rise, winding her way in and out among the trees and thorn bushes towards what might prove to be her salvation. The rain beat against her slim body, saturating her clothes, and she shivered uncomfortably when she paused a little distance away from what she had considered to be a farmhouse. What she saw was no more than a small cottage with what appeared to be a thatched roof, and she hesitated with uncertainty, but the light in the window beckoned, offering warmth and protection from the torrential rain and, overcoming her natural shyness, she approached the cottage with care and curiosity to peep in through the window.

The room was empty except for a dilapidated sofa and armchair arranged carelessly in front of the stone fireplace in which a log fire crackled lustily. On an old-fashioned cupboard against the wall stood a paraffin lamp, but there was no sign of a living soul.

Caroline was undecided as she stood out there in the rain, her clothes clinging to her body, and her wet, muddy shoes beginning to feel like frozen, damp leather encasing her feet. She longed for the warmth of the fire beyond the small wooden-framed window, but something held her back, and her body, stiff with the cold, was slow to respond to the warning that flashed through her mind.

She continued to hover beside the window, deciding too late to retrace her steps, for the next instant a heavy hand nearly wrenched her shoulder from its socket, and her torch fell from her chilled fingers to lie shattered at her feet. She was thrust against the concrete wall with a force that knocked the breath from her body, then her frightened eyes were staring up at the enormous and ominous-looking shadow looming over her.

'Who are you, and what do you want?' a deep, gravelly voice demanded harshly, and as the numbness of fear invaded her body she could do nothing except stare up at the sinister shape of the man towering over her menacingly. She tried to speak, but no sound passed her frozen lips, and she stood there shaking inwardly and outwardly in his grasp as he ordered gratingly, '*Answer me!*'

Caroline tried again, but her voice had become locked in her throat, and the man muttered an expletive that merely intensified her fear as he grasped her now by the scruff of her neck with an ungentle hand and marched her into the cottage.

She had never felt so frightened in all her life when she found herself standing there in the centre of the room which she had stared into through the window some moments before. She was shivering uncontrollably, but she dared not move closer to the fire; not while that enormous man in the dilapidated black raincoat clenched and unclenched his hands at his sides as if he was contemplating something drastic. Water was gathering in a little pool about her feet, and she was grateful, at least, to take the weight off her rubbery legs when he gestured her roughly into an upright chair against the wall farthest away from the warmth her shivering form so desperately craved.

Her captor removed his raincoat and slouch hat and hung them on a hook beside the door and, when he turned back to face her, she was more terrified than before. Hair the colour of a lion's mane fell in an unruly fashion across his broad forehead, and at least a week's growth of beard gave the rugged features a cruel, menacing appearance. A thick woollen sweater accentuated the width of his powerful shoulders, and faded denims clung to narrow hips and muscular thighs. He was the most strikingly virile man she had ever met and, if she had not been so afraid, she might have been impressed.

A rifle was propped up against the wall, but something told her that this man did not need such a weapon, for he looked quite capable of making use of those large hands if he needed to assert himself physically. He was standing before her, his legs apart, and his thumbs hooked into the waist band of his denims. Her eyes darted towards the door, but she knew that it would be futile thinking of escape.

'Now, let's have it,' he thundered at her. 'What were you doing lurking about outside my cottage?'

'I—I was looking for—for help,' Caroline explained, having difficulty in preventing her teeth from chattering. 'My car—my car is stuck down by—by the river.'

A frightening little silence followed her explanation, his razor-sharp eyes withering her inwardly, then he stepped forward to wrench the sodden cap from her head, and her damp hair tumbled down on to her slim shoulders.

'My God, you're a girl!' he exclaimed in rough surprise, taking in the wide grey eyes raised to his, and the sensitive, quivering mouth, then he demanded angrily, 'What in the name of all that's holy are you doing out on a night like this?'

'I—I lost my way, and now my car is stuck d-down by the river, and the river is in flood,' she explained, pushing an unsteady hand through her hair and feeling perilously close to tears.

'What's your name?'

'Caroline . . . Caroline Adams.' Her captor's attitude had become less menacing, but he had lost none of his alertness, and she could not deny that she was still fighting against the numbness of fear as she asked hopefully, 'Do you think you could help me get my car out of the mud? I thought I might return the way I came until I found another road which might lead me back to Matjiesfontein.'

'That won't do you any good,' he dashed her hopes. 'You'll have another bridge to cross before you reach a turn-off to Matjiesfontein, and it will be equally impassable.'

Her eyes widened in growing alarm. 'You mean I'm stuck here between two low-water bridges?'

'That's about it.'

'But what am I going to do?'

His unshaven face looked hard and angry as he stared down at her shivering form. 'You'll have to stay here.'

'Oh, but I can't do that,' she protested at once, not wanting to be in this frightening man's company longer than was absolutely necessary.

'You have no choice,' he told her gratingly. 'You either stay here, or spend the next couple of nights in your car.'

'Do you have a telephone?' she asked hopefully, clutching at the final straw.

'I'm afraid not,' he stated bluntly, then he jerked his thumb towards the fire. 'You'd better warm yourself. I'll be back in a minute.'

Caroline needed no second invitation, and she fell down on her knees directly in front of the log fire, forgetting her fears temporarily, and shivering with pleasure as the warmth slowly invaded her uncomfortably damp garments. She held her frozen hands out towards the fire, then combed them through her hair in an effort to dry it.

Heavy footsteps sounded on the wooden floor behind her, and she looked up over her shoulder to see her captor unfolding a blanket and holding it up like a shield between them.

'Get out of those wet clothes,' he instructed.

'I—I can't!' she cried, alarmed at the prospect of what he expected of her.

'For God's sake, child, it wouldn't be the first time I've laid eyes on the intriguing anatomy of the female species,' he rebuked her sharply, but when she rose unsteadily to her feet, he turned his head away with a faintly derisive smile about his mouth, and raised the blanket higher.

Cheeks flaming with embarrassment, she stepped out of her sodden shoes and peeled off her wet clothes, then the blanket was draped unceremoniously around her shivering form. She wished now that he would go away and leave her alone, but instead she found herself watching him drape her slacks, shirt, woollen jersey, and undergarments over the iron stand close to the fire and, mortified, she flushed. Her car keys slipped from the pocket of her slacks and, without a word, he stooped to pick them up off the floor and strode out of the cottage, pulling on his raincoat as he went.

Wrapped up warmly in the thick blanket, Caroline sat curled up on the large armchair beside the fire and assessed the situation as calmly as she could. She was clearly the unwanted guest of a man who frightened her considerably, while somewhere in this vast farming area Dennis and his parents waited in vain for her to put in an appearance. She had looked forward eagerly to this weekend for more reasons than one. She had hoped that Dennis and his parents would somehow be able to assist her with her pressing financial problems, but instead she was trapped between two estuaries of a river which might not subside for at least a few days unless the rain ceased overnight, and meanwhile she was still saddled with the problem of Maxwell Hilton, who was becoming impatient in his demands of repayment.

Her thoughts returned to her captor. Who and what was he? With that growth of beard and scruffy clothes he looked like a tramp, but there was something indefinable about him that suggested the opposite. He was a man used to having his orders carried out, which sug-

gested that he was a man of some authority. But what
was someone like that doing living out in the country
under such appalling conditions?

Puzzled and intrigued, Caroline forgot about her fears
for a while, and her heavy eyelids drooped until the
long golden lashes fanned her pink cheeks. The rhythm
of the rain against the window panes and the crackling
of the log fire was oddly soothing and, snuggling deeper
into the folds of the blanket, she promptly went to
sleep.

She had no idea how long she had slept, but she
awoke with a start when a fresh log was thrown on to
the fire. Her eyes, still heavy with sleep, fastened on to
the tall stranger towering over her, and her fears
returned with a rush. How long had he been away and,
more important, how long had he been standing there
observing her?

'I've towed your car out of the mud, and it's parked
at the back of the cottage,' he told her expressionlessly,
then he gestured toward her suitcase on the floor beside
her chair. 'I took the liberty of bringing it in for you,
and I suggest you change into something warm.'

He strode out of the room and had closed the door
behind him before she could rouse herself sufficiently to
thank him, but she hastily did as he had suggested, while
at the same time dispersing with the clothes which had
dried considerably in the heat of the fire. When her
bearded host entered the room once more she was
dressed in a fresh pair of slacks and a warm sweater,
and in the process of restoring a certain amount of order
to her hair by tying it back in a casual ponytail.

'You'd better drink this before it's cold,' he said,
placing a bowl of soup and several slices of buttered
bread on the low table before her.

'Thank you,' she muttered selfconsciously, slanting a wary glance at him. 'And thank you for rescuing my car as well.'

He did not acknowledge her thanks, but merely seated himself on the sofa opposite her chair while he lit his pipe, and his manner suggested that he was only barely aware of her presence.

Caroline was not in the least hungry, but the soup was tasty and filling, while the bread was deliciously fresh, and it was only when she set aside the empty dishes that she realised how hungry she had actually been. Except for the apple she had eaten for lunch on the way, she had not had a proper meal since the evening before, and she now felt wonderfully replenished.

On the sofa close to her chair her host was watching her through a screen of smoke, his eyes narrowed and intent upon her face. It made her feel oddly uncomfortable to be observed in this manner and, for want of something better to say, she asked hesitantly, 'Do you— do you live here alone?'

'Yes,' he confirmed bluntly without elaborating further, and she lapsed into an uncomfortable silence when she sensed that he disliked being questioned about himself. It was he who finally fired a question at her. 'Are you on holiday?'

'Sort of,' she replied vaguely, thinking how different the day had ended from what she had imagined.

She was the guest, by circumstance, of a man she had never met before, and for all she knew he could be a criminal in hiding from the police authorities. Her insides twisted into that familiar knot of fear at the thought as she observed him unobtrusively. He looked vaguely familiar, and not at all like a criminal, she decided, but how could she be sure of the latter?

'You're not very talkative, are you,' he interrupted her disturbed thoughts and, when she did not reply, an angry exclamation passed his lips. 'Look, whether we like it, or not, we're stuck here together until the bridges are passable, so we might as well pass the time in a reasonably social manner.'

Dubious as she was of her safety, his remark made sense, and she nodded slowly. 'I suppose so.'

He knocked out his pipe against the grate, filled it with fresh tobacco, and re-lit it, and only when it was burning to his satisfaction once again did he break the silence between them. 'What did you mean you're *sort of* on a holiday?'

'I'm between jobs, actually,' she explained, trying desperately to keep the nervous tremor out of her voice as the aromatic odour of pipe tobacco filled the room. 'The firm I worked for in Cape Town has closed down, and I'm hunting for another post at present, but . . .'

'I gather not many vacancies exist,' he filled in for her with remarkable understanding when she paused self-consciously.

'Not many, no,' she admitted reluctantly.

'Where were you travelling to at this time of night?'

'I was to have spent the weekend with my fiancé's parents in the Sutherland district, but I must have taken the wrong turning, and travelling in the rain held me up.'

He had peculiar greenish-yellow eyes, she noticed, and they travelled with swift alertness to her left hand before returning to her face.

'You're not wearing a ring,' he commented bluntly, and not quite knowing why, she found herself explaining,

'We were going to make our engagement known officially this weekend.'

'And now, instead, you're stuck here with me,' he concluded, and although she could not swear to it, she was almost positive she saw a gleam of mockery lurking in his eyes. 'Tell me about your parents.'

It was a command, and she reacted to it instinctively. 'My mother died when I was a baby. My father married again, but the marriage didn't last, and he died a year ago.'

'You have no one else?'

'No one except Dennis,' she answered quickly, and once again that suggestion of mockery lurked in his eyes.

'Dennis, I take it, is your fiancé?'

Caroline was getting a little tired of his third degree questioning, but she nevertheless nodded and said stiffly, 'Yes, he is.'

Those narrowed, thoughtful eyes observed her intently until a pulse began to jerk in her throat, and she looked away quickly to stare into the leaping flames in the grate. This man had made the most alarming impact on her from the moment he had confronted her in the rain outside his cottage. At first her emotions had been governed by fear, but now there was an awareness of a danger she could not put a name to. Despite his rough outward appearance, there was a distinct quality of breeding in the way he moved and spoke. It was confusing, but not at all comforting, and she cursed herself once again for not paying more attention to the directions Dennis had given her.

'How old are you?'

The question startled her out of her thoughts, and she answered almost automatically. 'Twenty!'

'My God, you're still a child!' he exploded, removing

his pipe from his mouth to frown down at it as if he wondered how it had got there.

'I'm not a child!' she protested indignantly, but a flush stained her cheeks when she caught his glance roaming over her slender yet shapely form with a deliberation that left her with the alarming sensation that she had been stripped down to her smooth skin.

'Very well, you're a young lady on the brink of womanhood,' he conceded mockingly. 'Does that make you feel better?'

Deciding it best to change the subject, she asked, 'How long do you think this rain will last?'

'A day—two days—who knows?' he shrugged carelessly, thrusting his pipe once more between strong white teeth.

'Surely there must be somewhere else I could go to?' she asked a little frantically now.

'If you're prepared to walk fifteen kilometres across rough country in this weather, yes,' he informed her dryly, then those catlike eyes pinned her mercilessly to her chair. 'You're afraid of me.'

'Can you blame me?' she asked at once with more bravado than she felt at that moment, but knowing that it would be useless denying her fears to this man with the probing eyes.

He did not reply, but merely regarded her intently for long, disturbing seconds before he rose to his feet and crossed the room to where his rifle stood propped up against the wall. Her heart was beating out a frightened tattoo when he picked it up and turned towards her, but her eyes were wide and startled moments later when he thrust the rifle into her hands.

'Does that make you feel any safer?' he demanded with a hint of sarcasm in his gravelly voice as he stood towering over her. 'It's loaded, and all you practically have to do is pull the trigger.'

She lowered her eyes to the deadly weapon in her hands, not knowing at that moment what to do, then she shook her head and held it out to him. 'I wouldn't really know how to use it.'

'Then you'll have to trust me,' he observed calmly, returning the rifle to its proper place against the wall, and for some peculiar reason she sensed approval in his manner.

He did not return to the sofa, but strode out of the room, and Caroline was left alone in front of the fire with the inexplicable sensation that he had taken some of the warmth with him. She shivered and glanced at the small clock on the mantelshelf. Ten o'clock! She had spent three hours in a strange cottage with a strange man, and although she was thankful for the warmth of his fireside, she had grave doubts about spending the night under the same roof with him.

Her troubled thoughts turned to Dennis, and she wished there was some way she could contact him, but it was a futile wish, and she knew it. She was trapped in a difficult situation from which there was temporarily no escape, and she would just have to make the best of it.

'Coffee?'

So deep in thought was she that she had not heard her host return, and she looked up with a start to find him extending a mug towards her. As she accepted it from him with a murmured thanks she could not help thinking that the reddish-gold of his beard in the firelight gave him a devilishly dangerous appearance, and she decided nervously that there was every possibility that he was exactly that when aroused—devilish and dangerous.

'What kind of work do you do?' he continued his questioning after resuming his seat by the fire and stretching his long legs out before him.

'Secretarial,' she said, and her voice sounded slightly stilted with anxiety, plus a certain amount of renewed fear.

'Are you good at it?'

'My employers thought so,' she replied simply, curling her fingers around the mug and raising it to her lips.

He stared broodingly into the fire while they drank their coffee in silence, and she sensed somehow that he was deeply troubled. She was tempted to question him, but some obscure force held her silent, and as the seconds ticked by and lengthened into minutes she found her interest quickening in this man who had plucked her threateningly out of the rain which was still beating with a force against the window panes.

Not wanting to disturb him, she sat quietly in her chair, but fatigue finally lined her eyelids with lead, and her head drooped on to her breast.

'You're tired,' a deep, pleasantly masculine voice filtered through the fog of her exhaustion and, picking up her suitcase, he instructed her to follow him.

He led her from the lounge, down a short passage, and into a bedroom which was sparsely furnished with no more than the bare necessities such as a bed, a dresser with a small mirror above it, and a wardrobe; none of which matched, and all of which had obviously been in use for many years.

'This is your room,' Caroline protested guiltily. 'I couldn't possibly——'

'Shut up and do as you're told,' he ordered brusquely, dumping her suitcase on the floor beside the bed, and straightening to his full, imposing height which dwarfed her considerably. 'I'll be quite comfortable on the sofa in the lounge, and there's a key in the lock of this door if you have any qualms about spending the night under the same roof with me,' he voiced her thoughts of earlier that evening, and guilt sent a flood of embarrassing warmth into her cheeks.

'You—you're very kind,' she murmured selfconsciously, turning towards the lamp he had placed on the dresser. 'Won't you be needing this?'

'I'll manage by the light of the fire,' he said abruptly, pausing in the doorway to glance back at her. 'The bathroom is to the left down the passage,' he informed her, and the next moment he had closed the door firmly behind him.

Caroline expelled the air from her lungs, realising for the first time how tense she had been, and her eyes went at once to the large key which protruded from the old-fashioned lock in the door. She crossed the room swiftly, but she hesitated when her fingers touched the cold metal. Was there really any need for her to lock herself in when he could have molested her at any time during these hours since her arrival on his doorstep?

She considered this for a moment, recalling Dennis's accusations that she was too trusting, but some inner sense told her now that she had nothing to fear from the man who had given up his bed for her, and her fingers fell away from the key without turning it in the lock.

Too tired to bother with her usual nightly toilet, she undressed, turned out the lamp, and crawled into bed and, to her surprise, her feet encountered the warmth of a hot water bottle between the sheets. It was an oddly considerate gesture for a man with such an outwardly rough appearance, she decided, and a smile curved her mouth as the remaining fragments of her fears disintegrated. He considered her a child after all, and perhaps it was best that he should.

It was a long, dark night, but Caroline slept deeply, and totally unaware of the fact that her host spent most of the night chewing on the stem of his pipe and staring broodingly into the fire.

The cottage was not as primitive as Caroline had imagined, and she discovered this the following morning when she ventured into the bathroom. A gas heater supplied hot water to the bath and shower, and the old-fashioned contraption in the one corner proved to be a flush toilet.

Bathed and dressed, she made up the bed and tidied the room, but her glance went persistently towards the window where she had drawn aside the floral curtains. The rain had ceased during the night, but the sky remained an ominous grey, and her hopes of getting away that morning plummeted swiftly.

Her host was in the kitchen, frying eggs and bacon over a gas stove, and he glanced briefly over his shoulder when she entered, his eyes skimming over her disinterestedly.

'Set the table,' he ordered, not bothering with the customary greeting, and obviously not in the best of moods. 'You'll find everything you need in the cupboard under the window.'

Caroline did as she was told, reacting instinctively to the command in his voice, and some minutes later they shared a stoically silent breakfast.

She observed him unobtrusively while they ate, and wondered what dark thoughts were crowding in behind his broad, frowning brow. Unshaven as he was, he was not at all what she would call attractive, for his high-bridged nose showed signs of having been broken at some stage in his life, and there was a hint of cruelty in the hard curve of his mouth.

The unexpected impact of his catlike eyes boring into hers was like a surging current of heat travelling along her nerves, and for several compelling seconds she could not look away. She was aware of him suddenly as a man, not merely her unwilling host who had frightened the life out of her the day before, and for the first time in her life she experienced a physical awareness that made the blood flow at a heady pace through her veins. When she finally managed to tear her eyes from his to pour their coffee, her pulse rate was jerky and her hands unsteady but if he noticed, he did not comment on the fact.

'Do you think your friend, Dennis what's-his-name, will be anxious about you?' he asked at length, breaking the strained silence between them.

'Naturally he'll be anxious,' she replied at once. 'And he'll be absolutely furious when he learns that it was all my own fault.'

'Because you took the wrong turning in yesterday's atrocious weather, or because he'll have to delay his announcement of your engagement?'

'Both, I suppose,' she admitted unhappily. 'He hates having his plans disrupted, and his instructions were so simple a child should have been able to follow them.'

Those straight, heavy brows rose in faint surprise. 'You don't think, then, that he'll send out a search party to look for you?'

'I really don't know what he'll do,' she confessed, biting her lip nervously, then she hastily changed the subject. 'Do you farm this land?'

'You don't like discussing your fiancé, do you?' he stated mockingly, clearing the plates from the table and piling them in the basin.

'I don't mind discussing Dennis,' she replied, getting up to help him, then she added daringly, 'You're the one who's always avoiding my questions about yourself.'

She thought for a moment that she had said the unforgivable, then his brow cleared, and he explained in that same mocking tone he had used before, 'I'm an uninteresting recluse, and I wouldn't want to bore a child like you with the story of my life.'

Was there a story? Caroline wondered curiously. Or was he what he seemed to be; a struggling farmer endeavouring to make ends meet? His hands were not the hands of a farmer, she concluded eventually. They were strong, capable hands, but they were uncalloused, and the nails were clipped and clean.

'I'll dry if you'll wash the dishes,' he interrupted her thoughts and, for a time, she shelved her puzzling queries to concentrate on what she was doing, but that was not easy with this disturbing man standing so close to her.

CHAPTER TWO

THE morning passed slowly for Caroline with nothing to do but sit around and hope the weather would clear sufficiently for her to continue on her journey. Her host's sullen, brooding silences did not encourage conversation either, and by midday she had become thoroughly bored with herself.

'I think I'll walk down and take a look at the river,' she told him when she found him packing a fresh fire in the lounge.

'You'll be wasting your time,' he told her without looking up from his task. 'I was there this morning and the river is still in full flood. The bridge is totally under water, and only a fool would risk crossing it.'

Frustrated with idleness, she asked exasperatedly, 'Isn't there anything I could do? Make lunch, or something?'

He looked up then, his peculiar eyes flicking over her from head to foot before he gestured her away with an impatient hand. 'There's cold meat in the refrigerator and there should be a loaf of bread left in the bin. You could make a few sandwiches and coffee if you like.'

His broad back was turned to her once more, and she stared hard at it for a moment before she walked out of the room. She could not quite make up her mind about this man, but perhaps he was not worth wasting her thoughts on.

Later, however, when they ate their sandwiches and drank their coffee in front of the lounge fire, she could not curtail her curiosity. 'Do you live here all the time?' she questioned him.

'What does it look like to you?' he counter-questioned, biting into his third sandwich.

'There are times when you seem to fit in, and others when you don't.' Caroline stole a sidelong glance at him, and explained thoughtfully, 'You have a cultured voice.'

'So have you,' he said, his eyes mocking her and, as always, he steered the conversation away from himself. 'Tell me about your father.'

'My father was an artist and a dreamer. He was totally unreliable, and careless with money, and . . .'

'He left you with the burden of his debt,' he concluded with surprising accuracy when she paused abruptly.

'I manage,' she shrugged, but in her heart she knew that it was a lie. Her dismal little room in a second-rate boarding house was proof of that. The only item of luxury she possessed was her small car, and that, too, was second-hand. It was a repossessed car which she had been lucky enough to get for a few hundred rand, and she had paid it off as quickly as she could, but that was before her father had died, leaving her with the tremendous responsibility of his debts.

'How long have you been out of work?'

'Two weeks,' Caroline replied, emerging abruptly from her thoughts and glancing hopefully out of the window. 'It hasn't rained all day.'

'If you're lucky you might get away from here tomorrow.'

Caroline laughed for the first time, and it was a soft, pleasurable sound that made her host glance at her with renewed interest as she said: 'You sound as anxious to be rid of me as I am to be on my way.'

'You're a very pretty girl, and I'm a man, not a saint,' he announced in a clipped voice, and when he noticed her startled glance resting on him, he gestured with his head towards the rifle which stood propped up against the wall beside the door. 'You could always carry that around with you if you feel that you might need protection.'

The mockery in his voice made her blush deeply, and embarrassment held her tongue in check for a considerable length of time, but when she found him observing her intently over the rim of his coffee mug, she said the first thing that came to mind in order to ease the tension.

'You haven't told me your name.'

'My name is not important,' he snapped, placing his mug on the table between them and getting to his feet.

'You know mine,' she accused as she watched him cross the room to stand staring out of the window.

The fire crackled during the ensuing silence, and she thought for a moment that she had angered him, but he turned eventually and smiled at her a little twistedly.

'Would you settle for John Smith?'

'No, I wouldn't, because I know that's not the truth,' she replied with inherent honesty and, regaining her courage, she added: 'I must call you something, and if you must be so secretive about it, then I'll have to choose a name for you myself.'

'That sounds intriguing,' he mocked her, taking out his pipe and filling it with care as he returned to the fireside. 'Tell me,' he said, resting a booted foot on the grate, 'what name would you choose for me?'

She observed him in silence until he had lit the pipe to his satisfaction, then she replied thoughtfully, 'You remind me of a restless, prowling lion, so I think I shall call you Leo.'

'Leo,' he repeated the name, his eyes narrowed and glittering strangely, then his laughter, deep, throaty, and harsh, filled the room. 'How very ingenious,' he remarked when he was able to control himself, then he was striding out of the room, and out of the cottage.

Caroline sat there for a long time afterwards wondering just why he had laughed so much. Was the name she had chosen so totally ridiculous, or had she unknowingly come close to the truth? She could not decide which, and finally gave up the effort to carry their plates and mugs through to the kitchen.

The cottage was empty and silent without the man she had decided to call 'Leo', and as the afternoon dragged on she went into the kitchen to search through the cupboards as well as the gas refrigerator. She had to do something or go crazy, she decided, and, hauling out a sizeable piece of steak and a few items of tinned food, she began to prepare the evening meal.

When Leo finally returned to the cottage shortly before dark that evening, Caroline had successfully camouflaged the fact that they were to sit down to a meal consisting mainly of tinned food, and she felt inordinately proud of her culinary efforts when her host walked into the kitchen and sniffed the air appreciatively.

'You've made yourself at home, I see,' he remarked a little dryly, pulling out a chair and seating himself at the table.

Caroline glanced at him anxiously. 'I hope you don't mind, but I had to do something to occupy myself.'

He did not reply, but his eyebrows rose in surprise when she set out their plates and dished up the tinned potatoes warmed up in a beefy sauce. The diced carrots, steak, and mushrooms followed, and when she sat down opposite him, he nodded slowly and smiled that now familiar twisted smile.

'Not bad,' he announced. 'Not bad at all.'

'I'm glad you think so,' she smiled across at him a little shyly, then neither of them spoke until their meal was finished and she had poured their coffee.

'Your fiancé is a very lucky man to have found someone like you,' Leo observed dryly.

'I think *I'm* very lucky to have found someone like Dennis,' she contradicted swiftly. 'I don't think he'll ever let me down.'

'Like your father did, you mean?'

His remark startled her, and she was instantly on the defensive. 'Please don't misunderstand. I loved my father very much even though I was aware of his failings.'

A gleam of mockery lit his eyes. 'Is that how you love your Dennis?'

'Dennis hasn't any failings that I know of,' she argued stubbornly and unwisely, for Leo was unmoved.

'All humans have failings, and my advice is that you should take a more critical look at this man you're planning to marry.'

'Your cynicism won't make me change my mind.'

'Perhaps not,' he concluded, 'but reality might.'

His remark troubled her for a considerable time after that, but, as before, she gave up trying to understand this extraordinary man who had given her shelter in the storm.

That night, beside the fire, she found herself thinking disturbingly less of Dennis, and far too much of the man seated a little distance from her. He sat smoking his pipe in silence, his eyes broodingly on the fire, but she had a peculiar feeling that every muscle in his long body was geared for action. He was a man of mystery; someone she had met only the day before, and yet there was something about him that drew her inexplicably towards him, a magnetic quality which was frightening as well as strangely exciting.

It was madness, she told herself, and she got up out of her chair with a feeling of agitation to kneel in front of the log fire. This way she did not have to look at him, but it did not diminish the fact that she was aware of him with every nerve and fibre of her being.

'Are you missing your lover?'

His voice startled her at first, then she cast him an indignant glance over her shoulder. 'Dennis is not my lover!'

'How long have you known him?'

'Two years.'

'And he's never made love to you?' he demanded with a gleam of derisive mockery in his eyes, and her cheeks reddened.

'We're both quite happy to wait until we're married.'

There was a tense little silence before he said dryly, 'I can see you're going to have a very dull, straightlaced life with your Dennis if he hasn't yet succeeded in awakening a little flutter of desire in you.'

'That's none of your business!' she exclaimed, inexplicably angry as she leapt to her feet, but his fingers snaked about her wrist with the unexpected speed of a reptile, and she was jerked unceremoniously down on to her knees at his feet.

'Do you love him?' he demanded, his eyes burning into hers.

'Of course I do!' she insisted, trying to free her wrist from his grasp, and frightened by the look in his eyes.

'He's good, kind, and dependable, and he would never do anything to harm me.'

'He is, in fact, everything your father was not,' Leo added, his lips pulled back in a sneer.

'My father has nothing to do with it,' she argued heatedly.

'I doubt that very much,' he laughed harshly, releasing her wrist and gripping her shoulders with a biting firmness until she could feel the burning heat of his hands through her sweater. 'I'm willing to bet that it was not a physical attraction that drew you towards Dennis, but his good, kind, dependable, stiff-necked character,' he accused, his voice slicing through her, angering her, and the most dreadful part of it all was that there was some truth in what he had said.

'You have no right to say such things,' she accused, her heart beating so fast now that it almost choked her. 'I love Dennis, and I'm going to marry him.'

'Love!' he snorted disparagingly. 'It's an overrated word, but make very sure of your feelings before you take that vital step.'

'But I *am* sure!'

'Are you?'

Those catlike eyes seemed to mesmerise her, and she sounded infuriatingly unsure as she heard herself say insistently, 'Yes, yes, I am!'

His masculine scent was all around her, invading her nostrils and stirring her senses until she felt herself shaking beneath his hands as she kneeled there before him. She was unable to wrench her eyes from his, and she was caught between fear and some terrible fascination.

'Do you tremble because you're afraid of me, or is there perhaps some other reason?' he questioned softly, and her gold-tipped lashes fluttered down to hide the confusion in her eyes when he added with a soft note of laughter in his voice, 'Let's find out, shall we?'

She was drawn up between his knees and, like someone in a hypnotic state, she allowed him to kiss her on her quivering lips. It was a light, explorative kiss, but it sparked off something within her that made her pulse rate soar alarmingly.

'Your Dennis is obviously not a very knowledgeable tutor in the art of kissing.'

His mocking statement made her draw back sharply, but his arms, like a vice, were clamped about her instantly, drawing her hard against him until her breasts hurt against the wall of his chest. Alert now to the danger of what was happening, Caroline tried to avert her face, but his beard scraped against her chin, and then her lips were being parted beneath the pressure of his mouth.

Caroline had never before been kissed with such a sensual intimacy, and she was totally unprepared for the alien sensations that clamoured through her until her limbs felt as though they had turned to water. Her hands clutched weakly at his shoulders in an effort to steady herself mentally, but touching him like that sent new sensations coursing through her. She could no longer think straight, and when, for the first time in her life, she knew the touch of a man's hand against her breast, she experienced the first stirrings of a wild, chaotic emotion that alarmed and excited her simultaneously.

When Leo finally released her she was breathless and flushed, and totally incapable of meeting his eyes while her heart still thudded wildly against her ribs. She rose shakily to her feet, and so did he, his hands steadying her as she swayed. His touch seared through her, and quite suddenly she was fighting against the mad desire to lean against him, and to feel again the crushing hardness of his body against her own.

Innocent as she was, she sensed the danger of prolonging this moment and, taking a pace away from him, she said unsteadily, 'I think I'd like to go to bed.'

'Is that an invitation?'

Her colour deepened and, to cover up her embarrassment, she said angrily, 'You've had enough fun at my expense, I think.'

He did not try to stop her when she walked out of the lounge, but she felt his eyes boring into her back until she was out of his sight. She undressed in the darkness and climbed into bed, but sleep evaded her for many hours while her mind recalled every detail of what she had experienced in the arms of a man whose existence she had not been aware of until the day before. She blushed with shame now at the thought of the intimacies she had allowed him, and she could not imagine what he must be thinking of her, but she had been like someone drugged and incapable of coherent thought.

Dennis had kissed her often in the past, but his kisses had never stirred her to such incredible depths, and never would he have dreamed of caressing her as intimately as this man had done. Caroline groaned inwardly at the memory, and prayed that she would be able to get away the following morning. She dared not stay much longer in this man's disturbing company if she wanted to retain her sanity.

She forced herself now to think of Dennis, of her love for him, and of how their friendship had grown into a warm, satisfying relationship. Marriage to him would afford her the quiet happiness she had always longed for, she told herself firmly, shutting out the sudden and unwanted doubts which invaded her mind. This madness she had experienced in another man's arms was something best forgotten, and she blamed it entirely on the circumstances which had brought them together.

It was with this thought that she finally went to sleep, but her dreams were confused and bewildering, and she was relieved when she awoke the following morning to see the sun shining in through the bedroom window. The grey, wintry countryside had been transformed into a paradise of green and gold, and she dressed and packed her suitcase hastily in anticipation of her departure.

Except for confirming that the river had subsided sufficiently for her to cross the low bridge, Leo was equally silent at the breakfast table, and it was only when he carried her suitcase out to her car that he spoke once again.

'Your car's fuel tank was rather low,' he said. 'I've put in ten litres, which should get you to where you want to be.'

'Thank you,' she smiled shakily, but gratefully. 'You—you've been very kind.'

'Have I?' he mocked her, and she lowered her eyes hastily in confusion as the memory of last night leapt to the surface of her mind.

'May I pay you for the petrol?'

'Forget it!' he snapped angrily, dumping her suitcase on the back seat of the Austin and holding the door open for her. 'It's time you were on your way.'

His obvious haste for her to leave was somehow hurtful, but she hid her feelings behind a careless laugh. 'Yes, I'm sure it is,' she agreed as she climbed into the car. and allowed him to close the door for her. 'I have a long way to go, and I shall have a lot of explaining to do when I reach my destination.'

A dark frown settled between his heavy brows. 'I don't advise that you tell your fiancé exactly where you've spent these last two nights.'

'Why ever not?' she demanded in surprise as she inserted the key in the ignition.

'He might not understand.'

Caroline stared up at him for a moment in thoughtful silence, then she said: 'I'm not much good at telling lies, and I think it would be best if I told everything exactly as it was.'

'I admire your taste for honesty,' he remarked with a cynical smile curving his mouth, 'but do you intend telling him about last night as well?'

'No, I suppose not.' Her colour rose as she bit her lip and looked away. 'That incident is best forgotten, I should say.'

'Will you be able to forget it?'

The question startled her, but she covered up her confusion hastily, and extended her hand towards him through the open car window. 'Goodbye ... Leo,' she said, using the name with a nervous little smile hovering about her soft mouth, but there was no answering smile on his lips when his large hand enveloped hers. 'I really do appreciate the fact that you gave me shelter when I needed it,' she thanked him.

'Take this with you,' he said abruptly, releasing her hand and producing a small white card on which he had printed a name and a telephone number. 'When you return to Cape Town I suggest you contact that chap. He'll have a job for you.'

'Harold Price,' she read the name out aloud, then she glanced up at him suspiciously. 'Is he a friend of yours?'

'A distant acquaintance, that's all, but you'll find him

helpful;' he assured her mockingly, and moments later she was driving away from him down the uneven track towards the road below.

She could see him in the rear view mirror. His hands were thrust into the pockets of his denims, and the early morning sun had nestled in his unruly hair. It was crazy to feel this way, she told herself, but it felt as if she were leaving a vital part of her behind.

In the daylight Caroline discovered where she had made her error in the storm, and she found the correct route without difficulty this time.

It was approaching ten-thirty that Sunday morning when she pulled up in front of the solid-looking farmhouse belonging to the Lindsays, and she had barely stepped out of her car when Dennis, lean, dark and furious, was at her side.

'Where in heaven's name have you been?' he demanded, his hands gripping her shoulders as if he wanted to shake her.

'I was——'

'I've been nearly out of my mind with worry,' he interrupted her explanation furiously. 'I've been in touch with almost every police station between here and Cape Town, but none of them could help us.'

'I can explain, Dennis,' she managed to say at last, but once again he interrupted her.

'Come and meet the parents first,' he said, taking her suitcase out of the car and ushering her towards the house with the wide verandah. 'You can explain later,' he added firmly.

Mr and Mrs Lindsay seemed nice enough on the surface, and they welcomed Caroline with what appeared to be a genuine warmth. She was shown to her room and given the opportunity to freshen up after her journey, then tea was served in the spacious living-room. It was while they were drinking their tea that Caroline received the opportunity to explain why she had failed to arrive on the Friday evening as planned.

A silence descended on the room when she had finished, but when she glanced enquiringly at Dennis, it was his mother's voice that erupted into the strained stillness.

'Do you mean to tell us that you spent two nights and a day alone with this—this man, and that you still have no idea who or what he is?'

Caroline shifted her glance from Dennis's thin, rigid features to the outraged, tight-lipped woman seated opposite her. 'He didn't tell me his name, and I didn't feel the need to insist that he should identify himself.'

'For all you know he could have been a criminal, or something worse,' Dennis intervened, and Caroline smiled at him with peculiar indulgence.

'I'm certain he's nothing of the kind,' she argued quietly.

'I hope, my dear, that you don't intend repeating this story to anyone else,' the older woman captured Caroline's attention once more.

'Why not, Mrs Lindsay?' Carline asked, forcing down her irritation. 'Nothing happened that I need be ashamed of.'

'Mother means——'

'I can speak for myself, Dennis,' his mother interrupted haughtily before returning her attention to Caroline, who was beginning to feel decidedly uncomfortable. 'We're well known in this district,' Mrs Lindsay continued, 'and if word should get around that my son's future wife spent so much time alone with a strange man in his cottage, no matter what the circumstances, then we shall never be able to look people in the eyes again.'

'But, Mrs Lindsay, I——' Caroline started to protest, but on this occasion it was her husband who interrupted.

'We believe you, of course, that nothing ... er ... happened between you and this ... er ... man, but you know how people speculate about such a situation.' Mr Lindsay smiled at her a little bleakly. 'People enjoy gossiping, and they never hesitate to add a few tails to their story which are often totally untrue.'

'The parents are right, darling,' Dennis intervened, patting her arm in what she felt was an impersonal manner. 'It would be best if this subject was never mentioned again.'

Caroline suppressed her growing anger for his sake, and nodded agreeably. 'If you say so, Dennis.'

'Good,' he said abruptly. 'Now, let's get something else over with.'

His hand dived into his jacket pocket, and before she had time to register what was happening, an elaborate diamond ring was slipped on to her finger.

The unpleasantness temporarily shelved, Caroline endeavoured to produce a certain amount of enthusiasm for the occasion, and although Dennis's parents made a show of congratulating them, Caroline sensed that they were not altogether thrilled with their son's choice.

Mr Lindsay opened a bottle of champagne at the luncheon table to celebrate their engagement, and everything seemed to be very jolly on the surface, but Caroline suddenly had the illogical desire to be back at the cottage sharing sandwiches with her bearded host in front of the log fire.

Dennis showed her around the farm that afternoon, but he was unusually quiet and uncommunicative, and the silences between them became lengthy and frequent as the afternoon progressed. He kissed her once beneath the shady acacia tree, but his lips were cool, and hers unresponsive.

That evening, when his parents had gone to bed, and they had been left alone beside the living-room fire, he drew her down on to the sofa beside him. Caroline went into his arms quite willingly and offered him her lips, but a little while later she sensed that they were both failing in their desperate attempts to inject a certain warmth into their embrace.

'Caroline, about this man . . .' he said at last, drawing away from her and lighting a cigarette.

'I thought we weren't going to discuss the subject again.'

'I know, but . . .' He blew a cloud of smoke towards the ceiling and turned his dark, enquiring gaze on her. 'Nothing happened, did it?'

Caroline stiffened with anger and disappointment. 'I didn't go to bed with him, if that's what you want to know.'

'I was merely asking, and there's no need for you to be so furious about it.'

'I'm not furious,' she argued quietly. 'I'm merely stressing the fact that, although I slept in his bed, he didn't join me there.'

'Were you together all the time?'

'Most of the time, yes.'

'I hope he didn't make any indecent suggestions to you?'

His suspicious attitude sent an upsurge of anger through her which she could no longer control, and her eyes were emitting sparks when she turned to face him squarely. 'The only suggestion he made was that I shouldn't tell you where I'd been, and I'm beginning to think he was right!'

'Why would he suggest that you should lie about where you've been if nothing happened between you?' Dennis demanded, avoiding her eyes now for some reason.

She stared at him for a moment and wondered at the curious lack of warmth within her at the sight of his lean, handsome features. It frightened her, this coldness for a man whose assistance and understanding she needed so desperately at that moment. She had hoped to discuss her pressing financial problems with Dennis and his family, but under the circumstances it seemed best to shelve the idea and, twisting her newly acquired diamond ring about her finger, she asked quietly, 'What is all this leading up to, Dennis?'

'We're going to be married, and I'd like to be sure of you.' He drew hard on his cigarette and blew the smoke out of the corner of his mouth as he glanced at her guiltily, 'Is that such a crime?'

'What you're really saying is that you would like to make sure that I'm still untouched sexually,' she remarked tritely.

'I wouldn't put it as crudely as that, but . . . yes,' he admitted grudgingly, and her opinion of him diminished a great deal more.

'Don't you trust me?' she asked unsteadily.

'I always thought I could in the past.'

'And you don't think so now, is that it?'

'Dammit, Caroline, can you blame me for wanting to be sure?' he demanded angrily, crushing his cigarette into the ashtray beside him. 'There's our family reputation to consider, and Mother said this evening that she's sure you're hiding something from us.'

'Your mother was right,' she snapped in defiance and anger when she managed to find her voice. 'What I haven't told you is that I found my reluctant host an interesting and intriguing person to be with, and there's something else too.' She drew a ragged breath and gripped her hands tightly in her lap. 'He kissed me last night, and I'd be lying if I said that I didn't enjoy it.'

There, it was said! And now Dennis could do with that bit of information as he pleased, she thought miserably as she lowered her gaze to her hands and blinked rapidly to disperse with the tears stinging her eyelids.

'He kissed you?' Dennis demanded incredulously.

'Yes,' she admitted. 'That's what I said.'

'My God!' he exclaimed in disgust. 'What else is still going to emerge from this mess, I wonder?'

'Only this,' she said unhappily, slipping the heavy ring off her finger and placing it on the sofa between them. 'I don't think I can marry you under the circumstances.'

'Caroline ...' Dennis was momentarily at a loss for words, then he said hesitantly, 'You're not serious, are you?'

'I'm afraid I am,' she said, raising her eyes to his, and in that moment she wondered why she should suddenly find him such a weakling in comparison to the man whose cottage she had shared in the storm. She was looking at Dennis, the man she had been so certain she loved, but it had taken a strange man's kisses to prove her wrong. Dennis was not for her, and no matter how much it hurt to realise it at that moment, she felt certain that in time she would come to terms with her decision. 'It's obvious that your family's reputation is more important to you than I am,' she said at length with a ring of bitterness in her voice, 'and who knows when someone might embarrass you all by digging up this indecent little incident in my past.'

'But——'

'Let's not discuss the subject further,' she interrupted hastily, rising to her feet and looking down at him a little sadly. 'It's over and done with, and I shall be leaving first thing in the morning.'

Dennis did not follow her from the room, and she was glad of that. She had endured enough for one day, and the tears were not far from spilling over on to her cheeks. She was going to have to face the future alone now, and it was with this disquieting thought that she undressed and climbed into yet another strange bed.

The situation did not alter for Caroline the following morning, and when she joined Dennis and his parents for breakfast it was obvious that he had already enlightened them about the termination of their embarrassingly brief engagement. They did not mention the subject, but it was clear to Caroline that Mr and Mrs Lindsay were relieved.

'Caroline, won't you reconsider?' Dennis pleaded with her eventually when he accompanied her out to her car. 'We were both over-reacting a little last night, don't you think?'

The long, sleepless hours during the night had left her cold and angry with herself that she could have been such a fool not to have seen through this man she had depended on so entirely, and she vented some of that anger on him now.

'I think I saw you last night for the first time as you really are. You're pompous, self-opinionated, and disgustingly narrow-minded, and I don't think I can spend the rest of my life conforming to your rigid style of living.'

'But we love each other,' he protested in what she knew to be a half-hearted attempt to make her change her mind, and she shook her head adamantly, and with a certain amount of amazement that her accusations had bounced off him so easily.

'No, Dennis, there's more to loving than this unemotional relationship that's existed between us. You've been a good friend, but that's really all.' She smiled up at him a little wanly. 'Thank your parents for their hospitality, and I'm sorry things have turned out this way.'

For the second time in twenty-four hours she was driving away from a man, but this time she was not heading towards a future built on unstable hopes and dreams. She was heading towards reality with a burden only she could bear, and there was very little comfort in that thought.

Caroline eased her foot off the accelerator when she approached the road turning off to the cottage. She was tempted beyond reason to see Leo just once more, but she rejected the idea almost instantly for fear of his mockery, and drove on at a steady speed towards Cape Town. She could depend on no one except herself in future, and she would have to make the best of whatever situation arose.

CHAPTER THREE

CAROLINE telephoned the employment agency only to be told that there were still no vacancies for someone with her secretarial qualifications. Her sigh echoed loudly in the telephone kiosk and, desperate as well as curious, she dialled the number on the small card that Leo had given her before her departure from his cottage.

'Protea Marine Engineering, good morning,' the pleasant voice of the switchboard operator rang in Caroline's ears, but for some obscure reason she lost her nerve at that moment, and replaced the receiver hastily without speaking.

Protea Marine Engineering. She had heard of it before. It was a privately owned company that built and repaired anything from a dinghy to the most luxurious yacht, and over the years it had palmed in contracts from all over the world to become one of *the* yacht building companies on the map.

Her mysterious host, it seemed, had contacts in high places. It puzzled and surprised her, and for the rest of the morning she was undecided about contacting Mr Harold Price of that most revered company. The employment agency had promised to telephone the moment something turned up, but could she afford to wait indefinitely?

In the tea-room around the corner from the boarding house, she ordered a sandwich and a cup of tea for lunch, and it was then that she made up her mind to go and see this man whose name was written in such bold print on the card between her agitated fingers.

A half hour later she was confronted by a guard at the security gate of Protea Marine Engineering. He enquired after her business, peered suspiciously into her dilapidated Austin, telephoned through to Mr Price, presumably, and finally let her through. Clearly defined arrows directed her towards the modern concrete and steel building that housed the office staff, and in the foyer she was once again directed by the enquiries staff to an office on the second floor.

Harold Price's secretary looked up sharply from her typewriter, and smiled enquiringly when Caroline entered her office. 'Can I help you?'

Caroline's fingers tightened nervously about the strap of her handbag. 'Would it be possible for me to see Mr Price?'

'In connection with employment?'

'That's right,' Caroline replied, moistening her dry lips.

'I don't think we have any vacancies at the moment, but I would like to confirm that with Mr Price.' The woman lifted the receiver on her desk and pressed the appropriate button. 'Mr Price, I have a young lady here enquiring whether we have any vacancies.' There was a brief pause, then the woman glanced quickly at Caroline. 'Your name, please?'

'Adams,' she supplied nervously. 'Caroline Adams.'

The woman repeated her name into the mouthpiece, her eyebrows rose fractionally at the reply she received, and then the receiver was replaced on its cradle.

'Mr Price will see you at once,' she said, indicating the door marked 'Personnel Manager'. 'You may go through.'

Caroline swallowed nervously and did as she was told, but a nerve was jumping at the corner of her mouth when she closed the door behind her in the bleak-looking office and turned to face the bald-headed man who had risen from behind the desk.

'Please sit down, Miss Adams.' He removed his dark-rimmed spectacles and waved with them towards the chair on the opposite side of his desk. 'I understand that you're seeking employment.'

'Yes, I am.' She perched herself on the edge of the chair and faced him anxiously when he had resumed his seat. 'Do you have any vacancies?'

'We have a vacancy in the accounts department which entails typing as well as clerical work.' He eyed her speculatively, and a little critically. 'Do you think you could cope?'

'Oh, yes,' she replied eagerly—a little too eagerly perhaps, and she blushed as she added shyly, 'I mean I'm sure I could manage.'

'Good,' he said abruptly, donning his spectacles and lowering his eyes to the papers before him.

'I have my credentials here, if you'd like to go through them,' Caroline offered, opening her handbag, but he waved them aside.

'That won't be necessary. You may start tomorrow at eight.' He scribbled something on a piece of paper and handed it to her. 'Take that along to one of my clerks who will take down all your particulars as well as discuss a salary, and so forth. You will also be issued with a temporary identification tag,' he added, and, when Caroline hesitated with uncertainty, he said abruptly, 'My secretary will show you the way.'

Caroline felt a little breathless as she rose to her feet. This was the oddest interview she had ever experienced, but she was not going to query the man's reasons for employing her in this haphazard fashion, and she smiled at him nervously.

'Thank you very much, Mr Price.'

'Don't thank me, Miss Adams,' he replied in a somewhat agitated fashion. 'I'm only doing my job to the best of my ability, and the rest is up to you.'

Caroline left the offices of Protea Marine Engineering less than a half hour later with a puzzled frown between her brows. Had she actually been employed, or was this a weird sort of dream from which she would soon awaken? She pinched herself just to make sure, and then only did she become excited about her good fortune.

At the end of her first week at Protea Marine Engineering she had practically forgotten her peculiar interview with the personnel manager. The weekend lay ahead of her, and when she reached the privacy of her dismal room in the boarding house, she realised for the first time how much she missed Dennis. It hurt to think of him, and of the happiness she might have shared with him, but she could never marry him now; not after the way he and his parents had behaved when they had heard of her forced stay in a remote cottage with a strange man for company. She had seen Dennis as he really was, and although she could not wipe out her feelings for him entirely, she knew that she could never live with a man who had shown so clearly that he did not trust her. Instead of being grateful that she had found shelter somewhere in the storm, he had been more concerned with his family's reputation, and that had been the final blow to sever their relationship.

Her thoughts turned unwillingly now towards the man whose kisses had awakened her to emotions she had never imagined before, and her pulse quickened alarm-

ingly at the memory. It was unlikely that they would
ever meet again; not unless she travelled all that way to
his cottage, and naturally, she would never dream of
doing anything of the kind, but . . .!

She pulled herself together and decided to have a
quick bath before all the hot water had been depleted.
It was ridiculous, this preoccupation with a man she
actually knew nothing about, she told herself fiercely,
but his bearded face had intruded into her thoughts on
so many occasions during this past week that she was
beginning to feel haunted.

Caroline had barely sat down at her desk on the
Monday morning when a slender, red-haired woman
entered the office and approached the desk nearest to
Caroline's.

'Hello, I'm Margery Doyle,' she smiled at Caroline.
'You're new here.'

'Yes,' Caroline nodded, judging her age somewhere
between thirty and forty. 'I'm Caroline Adams.'

Margery pulled out her chair and sat down behind
her desk with a sigh. 'I've just returned from a well-
earned holiday and, believe me, I'm not in the mood for
work.'

'It will be a long time before I can even think of going
on a holiday,' Caroline laughed lightly. 'I've only been
here a week, and I'm still trying to find my way around
the office.'

'Stick close to me, my dear, and I'll teach you all
there is to know about the work,' Margery promised.

Caroline liked her instantly, and during the course of
the morning she discovered that Margery Doyle was a
veritable hive of information concerning the work as
well as the people they worked with.

During lunch in the staff canteen, Caroline said tentatively, 'I heard someone calling you "Mrs Doyle", but you're not wearing a ring.'

'I'm divorced,' she said at once, a look of distaste flashing across her face. 'And I don't intend being caught in the same trap twice.'

Caroline stepped swiftly off the subject on to another. 'Have you been working here for many years?'

'I've been here since before the Lion took over the business from his father five years ago.'

'The Lion?' Caroline laughed, eyeing her curiously.

'The big chief's name is Gustav de Leeuw,' Margery explained. 'De Leeuw—The Lion. Get it?'

'Oh, yes,' Caroline nodded, growing thoughtful. 'I haven't met him yet, I don't think.'

'You won't either,' said Margery, spearing a piece of cucumber with her fork and popping it into her mouth. 'The Lion has his own private entrance to the building, and a private lift that takes him up to his lair on the sixth floor. He seldom sees anyone except the heads of departments.'

'Do you mean you've never seen him?' Caroline asked incredulously.

'Oh, I've seen him a couple of times driving off in his silver Jaguar, and I've seen his photograph in the newspapers occasionally, but I've never met him personally,' Margery told her. 'He keeps very much to himself, but I believe he's a tyrant when crossed.'

'You make him sound frightening,' Caroline remarked, unable to suppress the little shiver that shot up her spine.

'He's very fair in his dealings with the staff, and I can vouch for that, but there's not a soul who doesn't tread softly when the Lion's on the prowl.'

Caroline decided then and there that she did not like what she had heard of the head of Protea Marine Engineering, and she was secretly relieved at the knowledge that their paths were unlikely ever to cross.

It was at the end of her first month at P.M.E. (as everyone called it) that Caroline was once again forced to give her urgent attention to her problems. She arrived at her boarding house one evening to be told that she had a visitor waiting to see her in the small private lounge, and fear chilled the blood in her veins when she saw the man in the grey suit and red shirt rising from the chair which faced the door.

'Mr Hilton!'

'Good evening, my dear.' Maxwell Hilton's dark eyes darted up and down the length of her, then he crossed the room towards her. 'You look charming, as always, Caroline.'

'Why are you here?' she demanded, unable to hide her dislike as she watched him close the door and turn to face her once more.

'You know the answer to that as well as I do,' he replied smoothly with that detestable smile lurking about his thin mouth. 'My friends are no longer happy with the arrangement that they receive their money in small instalments. They want it *all*, and in hard cash.'

'I told you before, Mr Hilton, that I shall need more time. Seven thousand rand is a large amount for me to raise, and——'

'Why don't you admit that it's impossible for you to do so?' he interrupted in that suave manner of his. 'You have nothing to offer as security, my dear, and that's the problem, but I've come here today to offer you a solution.'

'A solution?' Caroline echoed suspiciously. 'What solution?'

He took his time lighting a cheroot, his thin, bony hands cupping the lighter, then he blew out a cloud of smoke and observed her through narrowed, hateful eyes. 'I shall give you another two weeks, and if, in that time, you can't raise the money, I shall pay your debt for you.'

'*You*'ll pay it for me?' she demanded incredulously. 'You mean you'll pay it, and then allow me to pay you back monthly as I've done in the past?'

'No, my dear Caroline,' he smiled calculatingly, 'I shall not demand the cash from you.'

'What do you mean?' she asked, holding her breath.

'There are other means with which a pretty girl like yourself can repay a man like myself.'

Revulsion swept through her to become lodged in her throat, momentarily choking her, then she cried furiously, 'Get out of here!'

His thin-lipped smile faded at once, and his attitude became menacing. 'I'll go, but don't forget that you have two weeks in which to find the money. If you don't,' he added threateningly, 'I shall write out a personal cheque, and exact payment in my own way.'

Caroline felt sick to the very centre of her being when the door closed behind him and, ashen-faced, she remained in that sparsely furnished lounge until she had regained her control sufficiently to climb the stairs up to her room.

Two weeks, he had said. Two weeks in which to beg, borrow or steal seven thousand rand, and heaven only knew how she was going to manage it.

During the week following Maxwell Hilton's visitation, fear motivated her once again into approaching several banks and finance companies, and they all turned her away regretfully, but firmly. As she had nothing to offer as collateral they could not give her a loan, and that was all there was to it.

On the Wednesday, a week after receiving Maxwell Hilton's revolting offer, Caroline was having lunch with Margery in the canteen when the older woman pinned her down with her green glance and said gently, 'My dear, I haven't wanted to pry, but something has been troubling you this past week. If there's anything I could do to help, then please tell me.'

'Oh, Margery, I only wish you could help,' Caroline sighed, pushing aside her untouched lunch and settling for a cup of tea.

'Try me.'

Caroline stirred her tea and placed the teaspoon carefully in the saucer before her troubled glance met Margery's. 'I need to raise seven thousand rand before next Wednesday.'

Margery's eyes widened considerably and she whistled softly in an unladylike fashion. 'My dear child, whatever for?'

Caroline explained as briefly as possible, and ended with, 'So you see, if I can't raise the money, then . . .'

'Then this Maxwell Hilton will reap payment in his own disgusting manner,' Margery filled in for her when she paused. 'I understand.'

'There's no way I can get hold of that kind of money, and I just don't know what I'm going to do.'

'I could help you with two thousand,' Margery offered, 'but that still leaves five thousand rand that you must find somewhere.'

'You're terribly kind, Margery, but——' Caroline bit into her quivering lower lip. 'Oh, I wish I were dead!'

'Don't say that!' the older woman reprimanded

sharply, then she reached across the table and gripped Caroline's arm lightly. 'Look, I'll ask around a bit and see what I can come up with before next Wednesday.'

'Would you really?' Caroline asked hopefully.

'I can't promise anything,' Margery warned, 'but I'll do my best.'

'Thank you,' Caroline sighed, blinking away her tears of relief at having been able to share her problem with someone.

They had barely started work that afternoon when the telephone on Margery's desk rang shrilly and, after answering it, she extended the receiver towards Caroline. 'It's for you.'

'Miss Adams?' Harold Price's voice exploded in her ear when she had taken the receiver from Margery. 'You're to go up to Mr de Leeuw's office at once. Drop everything, and don't waste time—Mr de Leeuw dislikes being kept waiting.'

'Yes, Mr Price,' Caroline replied in a voice that sounded stilted with a new kind of fear, 'I—I'll go at once.'

The line went dead, and Caroline's hand was shaking when she replaced the receiver on its hook.

'What's the matter?' Margery wanted to know when she glanced up into Caroline's white face.

'Mr de Leeuw wants to see me.'

'The Lion?' Margery almost shouted out her incredulity. 'My God, Caroline, what have you been up to now that you should be summoned to his lair?'

'Heaven only knows, but——' She bit her lip nervously. 'Say a little prayer for me, will you?'

'You can count on that,' Margery assured her. 'And . . . good luck!'

Caroline's brain was working at a frantic pace when

she took the lift up to the sixth floor. In a matter of seconds she had gone over every aspect of her work, searching desperately for a reason why she should be summoned into the Lion's revered presence, and finding none. Surely, if it had something to do with her work, he would have approached the head of the accounts department? Was that not what Margery had told her? That Gustav de Leeuw dealt only with the heads of departments?

When she finally reached the sixth floor she relinquished her efforts to find an answer for this puzzling development, but her insides were nevertheless shaking uncontrollably when she entered the office at the end of the passage.

'Miss Adams?' the grey-haired woman behind the desk enquired in an impersonal voice.

'Y-yes,' she stammered, trying to control the hammering of her frightened heart.

The woman indicated the door to her left, and Caroline approached it with a great deal of hesitancy. Beyond it the Lion awaited her, and, terrified beyond reason, she glanced back at the woman seated behind the desk.

'Don't keep him waiting,' was the reply to her silent plea for help and, taking a deep, steadying breath, she knocked lightly and entered.

The office was large and airy, and the furnishings were modern, but Caroline's frightened eyes were riveted to the man who stood silhouetted against the window with his broad back turned towards her. The smell of cigar smoke filtered her way, but the man in front of the window remained where he was as if unaware of her presence. She wondered suddenly whether she should clear her throat, or something, to attract his attention, but her throat felt so tight that she was certain not a sound would pass through it.

The silence continued to gnaw away at her already shattered nerves until, unable to stand it a moment longer, she swallowed convulsively and managed to whisper hoarsely, 'Mr de Leeuw?'

He stirred then, and turned to face her, but it was only when he approached his desk that she was able to see him clearly. Her heart missed a few beats as she blinked and stared, and then, as the room tilted dangerously about her, she gasped incredulously, 'You!'

Her legs threatened to cave in beneath her and, without waiting for a second invitation, she sat down heavily in the chair he had indicated while he lifted the receiver of the telephone system on his desk and stabbed at one of the numerous buttons.

'Mrs Franklin, I don't wish to be disturbed for the next hour,' that deep, familiar voice instructed, and then the receiver was dropped on to its cradle.

Caroline stared at the mane-like hair which was now trimmed neatly against the proud head and brushed back severely, then her bewildered gaze travelled to the catlike eyes, and the clean-shaven, ruggedly handsome features. This was the man in whose cottage she had sheltered, and yet he was a total stranger to her. The casual clothes and unsightly boots had been replaced by a dark, impeccably tailored suit, and expensive leather shoes. His white silk shirt contrasted heavily with his tanned complexion, and his sober grey tie was held in place with a diamond pin. To complete the confusing transformation from struggling farmer to flourishing businessman, there was a cigar smouldering between his fingers instead of the pipe she had become accustomed to associating with the image which had haunted her waking and sleeping hours during the past weeks.

'Well?' he demanded with a sardonic gleam in his eyes when he walked round his desk and seated himself behind it in his padded swivel chair. 'Have you nothing to say?'

Caroline knew she had been staring rudely, but suddenly she did not care, and an uncontrollable anger finally surged through her and loosened her tongue. 'I understand now why you found it so amusing when I named you Leo, and I also understand why Mr Price behaved so oddly when I came to see him about a job.' Her colour faded as her mind assimilated the shocking events of these past few minutes, and she lowered her face into her trembling hands. 'Oh, lord, I can imagine what he must have thought!' she moaned in a muffled voice.

'You're concerned about your reputation?'

The cynicism in his voice made her look up sharply. 'Naturally I'm concerned.'

Their glances clashed, and held, then he stated mockingly, 'I notice that you're still not wearing a ring.'

'I broke off my engagement.'

'Why?'

'Personal reasons,' she replied stiffly.

'You mean your Dennis didn't believe you when you told him that your virginity was still intact after spending almost the entire weekend alone with me,' he stated mockingly, and her colour deepened with embarrassment.

'That was one of the reasons, yes,' she admitted, lowering her eyes to her tightly clenched hands in her lap.

An uncomfortable little silence hovered between them, then he asked harshly, 'Is that all you're going to tell me?'

Caroline raised her glance warily. She might have been able to pour her heart out to him as the man she had named Leo, but at that moment the situation was vastly different. This man was Gustav de Leeuw, the Lion of Protea Marine Engineering, and the man who was feared yet respected by all who worked for him.

'Forgive me, Mr de Leeuw,' she said at last with a touch of nervousness and reverence in her voice, 'but I don't think my personal life concerns you.'

'You're wrong,' he barked at her, taking his cigar out of his mouth and placing it in the marble ashtray on his desk. 'Your personal life concerns me very much.'

Caroline blinked and stared at him a little stupidly. 'I don't think I understand.'

He pushed back his chair and walked across to the window to stand in the same position she had found him when she had entered his office. With his back turned towards her he started to speak, and the breath seemed to be squeezed out of her lungs with every word he uttered.

'Your father, Vincent Adams, died a year ago,' he said. 'The death certificate stated that he died of a coronary thrombosis, but in certain circles it's said that he drank himself to death. He lived on credit, and gambled away whatever cash he had had, and more, but instead of allowing his debts to die a natural death with him, your pride made you undertake repayment. You sold the cottage at Hout Bay to settle his accounts, but that left you with a gambling debt of eight thousand rand, of which, I understand you still owe seven thousand.' He turned and walked towards her then, his eyes pinning her helplessly to her chair. 'My information is correct, is it not?'

'How—how do you know all this?' she managed at

last in a voice that was no more than a whisper.

'I had you investigated.'

His blunt statement made her sit up rigidly in her chair. 'You had me *what?*'

'You heard me,' he said, seating himself on the corner of the desk and folding his arms across his chest.

'But why?' she demanded confusedly, staring a long way up into his rugged face.

'I'll explain later,' he said brusquely, his eyes holding hers captive. 'I'm told that a certain Maxwell Hilton paid you a visit a week ago. Is that correct?'

Caroline squirmed inwardly beneath his compelling gaze as she asked a little defiantly, 'What don't you know?'

'Do you have the seven thousand rand to keep him at bay, or do you intend giving in to his demands?'

'If you mean do I intend becoming his mistress, then the answer is "no",' she replied at once, distaste curving her soft mouth. 'I haven't the money to pay him, but I'd rather die than have him touch me.'

'That's what I wanted to hear,' he said, smiling that faintly mocking smile she remembered so well as he resumed his seat behind his desk. 'Now you and I can talk business.'

Caroline glanced at him suspiciously. 'What business do we have to discuss?'

Gustav de Leeuw held the flame of his gold cigarette lighter to the tip of his cigar, and only when he was satisfied that it was burning to his satisfaction did he answer her query.

'For reasons which I shall explain later, I must produce a wife before the end of this month. If you oblige me in this respect, then I shall see to it that Maxwell Hilton never troubles you again.'

Caroline stared at him in shocked disbelief, her colour coming and going in rapid succession. She tried to tell herself that she had not heard him correctly, but his words echoed repeatedly through her mind until she knew that this was not so.

'Are you asking me to marry you?' she asked incredulously when she had managed to find her voice.

'I am.' His eyes, glittering hard through the cloud of cigar smoke, never left hers. 'Marry me, and in return I'll pay your father's gambling debts.'

'Surely there must be someone you care for who would marry you?' she questioned protestingly.

'I enjoy my freedom,' he said abruptly. 'The women I know would want to make it a permanent arrangement, but with you I'm in a position to stipulate that the marriage ends as soon as certain parties are satisfied that I'm legally married.'

'What you're saying is that you don't mind using a nonentity like myself to serve your own ends,' she concluded angrily.

'That could cut both ways if you accept.' A cynical smile curved his hard mouth. 'Are you tempted?'

Caroline was tempted, *yes*. She was tempted to tell him to go to the devil, but she hesitated. He was offering her an avenue of escape from the clutches of Maxwell Hilton, and she was desperate enough not to ignore his offer outright. There was Margery, too, who was trying to help her in some way, and she had to await the results before she considered committing herself to this man in any way.

'I shall need time to consider your proposal,' she said at last in a shaky voice.

'You have until next Wednesday to find the money owing to Hilton. I'll pick you up at seven on the Tuesday evening, and then you can give me your answer over dinner.'

'Very well,' she nodded, wringing her hands nervously in her lap.

'You may go,' he dismissed her abruptly, but when she reached the door his authoritative voice halted her. 'Just a minute!'

'Yes?' she questioned, a nerve jerking at the corner of her mouth as she turned to face him, and he got up out of his chair to walk towards her.

'Can I rely on your silence?' he demanded, towering over her in a way that made her heartbeats quicken in that odd manner.

'You can,' she replied at once, 'but what do I say when people demand to know why I was called to your office?'

'I'm sure you'll think of something,' he smiled down at her mockingly, then he opened the door and stood aside for her to pass through it.

CHAPTER FOUR

THE lift took Caroline smoothly down from the sixth to the first floor, but she was in a dazed, confused state, and she was hardly aware of what she was doing, or where she was going. Her insides were shaking, and her mind was in a feverish whirl, but when she finally sat down behind her desk she had the curious sensation that she had lived through some sort of nightmare.

'Well?' Margery asked, eyeing her curiously. 'What did the Lion want with you?'

Caroline pulled herself together with a start, and said guiltily, 'I'm sorry, Margery, but it—it's a confidential matter I can't discuss yet.'

Margery's glance narrowed speculatively. 'Did it have anything to do with the seven thousand rand you require?'

'In a way, yes,' Caroline admitted, adding hastily, 'but I would still appreciate it if you could help me raise the amount.'

'I did say I'd do my best.'

'Thank you, Margery.'

Caroline hid her confusion and her fears behind a smile that grew dimmer as the days passed and lengthened into a week. She felt like someone caught between two fires, and the one was more deadly than the other. If she had to choose between the two offers she had received, then she would choose marriage to Gustav de Leeuw in preference to selling herself to Maxwell Hilton, but meanwhile she was pinning her hopes on Margery

Doyle coming up with a solution which would not necessitate anything as drastic as marriage to a man who was even more of a stranger to her now than he had been before.

She went to work on the Tuesday morning with a leaden feeling in her heart. Something told her that the situation was not going to be resolved as she had hoped, and she needed to take only one look at Margery's face to know that her suspicions had been correct.

'My dear, I've been just about to everyone I can think of, but——'

'I understand,' Caroline interrupted quietly with the smile she had been forced to wear those past few days. 'You've been very kind to trouble yourself with my problems, and I do appreciate it.'

'But what are you going to do?' Margery asked anxiously in a lowered voice as the rest of the staff filtered into the office.

'There is another solution which I hoped to avoid, but I'll tell you about it tomorrow.'

Margery eyed her suspiciously. 'You're not going to give this Hilton man what he wants, are you?'

'Not if I can help it,' Caroline whispered fiercely.

'Thank God for that,' Margery sighed. 'But what——?'

Caroline waved her to silence. 'Be patient a little longer. You'll know soon enough.'

They went to their respective desks and settled down to work, but Caroline found great difficulty in concentrating that morning with her dinner appointment hanging like the Sword of Damocles over her head. It seemed as if she would have no option but to marry the Lion in order to escape the revolting Maxwell Hilton. The Lion needed a wife, for some reason she still had to discover, and she needed the money to buy herself out of a difficult situation. It was not exactly the best reasons for venturing into a marriage, but as a business proposition it was tempting.

Caroline spent the entire day talking herself into a state of bravado, but when Gustav de Leeuw arrived at the boarding house that evening to collect her, she was a bundle of nerves and filled with dire misgivings.

He did not take her to a restaurant as she had expected, but to his gabled home in Constantia. 'We'll have more privacy there,' he had explained abruptly, and she had shrunk farther into the corner of her seat in the dark interior of his luxurious car.

His home was impressive and furnished with priceless antiques, but to Caroline, who was unused to such luxury, it was a frightening, instead of a pleasurable, experience, and she felt tonguetied and awkward in her cheap chiffon dress which had been the only suitable thing she could find to wear that evening.

They dined in a room leading off the main dining hall with servants coming and going discreetly, but Caroline was too nervous to be aware of what she was eating, or whether she had eaten anything at all while she sat facing the Lion across the length of the oak table. She was lured into conversation on several occasions, and although she tried very hard to imagine herself back at the cottage with him, she seemed to lose her power of speech whenever her gaze fell on her austere, autocratic host who was observing her intently with those peculiar eyes of his. At the cottage she could have placed herself on a level with him, but her host for this evening was far above her in every respect, and it puzzled her that he should have selected her to be his wife for whatever purpose he had in mind.

She was offered more wine after the last course was served, but she refused adamantly. Her head was already beginning to spin from too much wine, and too little food, and she dared not have more if she did not want to disgrace herself.

'Forgive me for asking,' she said at last when her curiosity could no longer be suppressed, 'but what were you doing in that remote cottage in the country?'

'The cottage is on land that belongs to me,' he explained. 'The actual farmhouse is beyond the river, but I have a manager living there who takes care of the place for me, so whenever I go there I stay in the cottage. I enjoy my privacy, and the peace and quiet of the country is ideal when I need to deliberate about something important.'

'I understand,' she murmured, realising now just how much of an inconvenience she must have been to him during her stay there.

'Do you understand, I wonder?' he remarked thoughtfully, and her heart behaved oddly at the faint smile that curved his mouth.

'I'm trying to.'

A silence descended on the room as their eyes met and held, and Caroline experienced the breathless sensation of being suspended over a deep chasm.

'Let's stop beating about the bush,' he shattered the silence abruptly. 'What have you decided?'

'Why do you need to have a wife so urgently?' she counter-questioned warily.

His jaw hardened resolutely. 'That remains a personal matter until I have your affirmative answer.'

'I haven't much of a choice, have I?' she pointed out miserably.

'You do have a choice,' he contradicted harshly. 'It's

either Hilton or myself.'

'That's exactly what I meant,' she stated with a note of helpless urgency in her voice. 'I told you I'd rather die than give in to Maxwell Hilton's demands, and that leaves only you I can turn to for protection and assistance.'

'Then you agree to marry me?' he asked unnecessarily with not a flicker of emotion crossing his face.

Caroline hesitated, but they both knew that there was only one answer she could give, and she gave it, albeit reluctantly. 'Yes, I agree to marry you.'

'Good,' he said abruptly, pushing back his chair and rising to his feet. 'Let's go through to the living-room, then I'll explain the situation to you.'

In the living-room, with its rosewood and stinkwood furnishings, and wine-red drapes, she seated herself in an upright, intricately carved chair and waited while he lit a cigar. A fire burned in the grate of the stone fireplace, warming the spacious room, but Caroline trembled with nerves and an uncommon coldness that clutched at her heart. She looked up enquiringly as Gustav passed her chair to stand with his back to the fire and, as their eyes met, he began his lengthy explanation.

'My mother was a sickly woman who died when I was five, and my father later married Isobel Findlay when I was twelve. She was a widow with a three-year-old son, Russell.' He paused to frown down at his cigar before continuing. 'My father had always ruled everyone, including my mother, with a rod of iron so to speak, but Isobel somehow managed to twist him around her little finger. She persuaded him to adopt Russell so that he would bear the family name, and then she set about convincing my father that I was not worthy of my inheritance. The result was that, when my father died two years ago, Isobel inherited this house, a twenty-five per cent share in the business, and a vast sum of money with which she took herself and Russell off to Namibia where they'd originally come from.'

'You inherited the business, though,' she remarked sympathetically, but she knew that sympathy was the last thing that Gustav de Leeuw would ever want.

'I inherit the business on condition that I'm married exactly two years after my father's death, yes.'

'But that's unfair!' Caroline could not help exclaiming.

'I'm partially to blame for it,' he frowned down at her. 'I never made a secret of the fact that I preferred my freedom, and in his later years my father became obsessed with the idea that the business should remain in the family. As there was no likelihood that I would produce an heir in my unmarried state, Isobel made use of this fact to convince my father that Russell would be a more likely candidate for producing an heir; hence the stipulation in the will,' he added with a touch of cynicism.

'I presume your stepbrother is married?'

'Oh, yes,' he said, smiling that twisted smile that seemed to pierce her heart. 'Isobel saw to that the moment they arrived in Namibia. He was married last year, and I understand that there's a child on the way— which means, of course, that they've made doubly sure of winning this battle.'

'What happens when—when our marriage is dissolved?' she wanted to know. 'Won't the stipulation in the will still apply?'

'No,' he shook his head, and she saw for the first time the suggestion of grey against his temples. 'The will states that, to inherit Protea Marine Engineering, I must produce absolute proof of my marital status on the stipulated date, and that's all. It doesn't state that I must remain married for the rest of my life.'

'I see.' Caroline lowered her eyes to her tightly clenched hands in her lap, and saw the bones shining white through her skin. 'On what date will they require this proof of your marriage?'

'On the fifteenth of September.'

'But that's only in about two months' time,' she protested, glacing up at him suspiciously. 'I thought you said that you had to be married before the end of this month?'

'That's correct,' he said, stubbing out his cigar and thrusting his hands into the pockets of his dark pants. 'Isobel will be arriving here in a week's time, and no doubt Russell and his wife, Nicola, will be accompanying her. She wants to be here in plenty of time to prepare for what she considers is rightly her son's inheritance and, naturally, she wants to make sure that I'm still unattached.'

'You plan to dampen their eagerness by producing a wife, is that it?' Caroline enquired a little wryly.

'You could say so, yes,' he admitted thoughtfully. 'I have an idea they're running out of funds, and if my plans eventually succeed I shall not only own Isobel's shares in the business, but I shall also possess my family home once again.'

He had mentioned plans, and she wondered suddenly just what part she would have to play in the execution of these plans to regain his rightful inheritance.

'What happens now?' she asked nervously.

'I take you back to your respectable boarding house, and you leave Maxwell Hilton, as well as all the other arrangements, to me.'

His authoritative tone did not invite arguments of any nature, and she lapsed into an abject silence that lasted until he parked his car in the silent street outside the building where she rented a room.

'There's one favour I'd like to ask you,' she began tentatively, turning in her seat to face him. 'May I tell my friend Margery Doyle about—about our decision? She's been good to me these past weeks, and I wouldn't like her to receive the news from elsewhere.'

His eyes glittered strangely in the street light that shone into the car, and she thought for a moment that he would refuse her, but then a flicker of a smile touched his stern mouth. 'You may tell her if you wish.'

'Thank you,' she whispered gratefully, and then he was helping her out of the car and escorting her towards the brick building where an unshaded globe lit up the entrance.

'I'll see you tomorrow,' he said once she was safely inside, and moments later she saw him drive away at speed.

It was not until Caroline was lying in her bed that night that the implications of her decision struck her with a numbing force. To escape the clutches of one man, she had agreed to deliver herself into the hands of another whom she had feared for some reason since the moment they had met that stormy night outside his cottage. Their marriage was to be a business arrangement; he would pay off her debt if she posed as his wife, but when she recalled his kisses on that last night in his cottage, she began to have grave doubts about the wisdom of her decision to marry him. Could they maintain a platonic relationship while living together under the same roof for a number of weeks?

Frightening thoughts came to mind, but she thrust them aside forcibly, and went to sleep, but she slept fitfully, and awoke hollow-eyed the following morning before the sun had risen over the city.

'What are you going to do about Maxwell Hilton?' was the first thing Margery Doyle asked when she walked into the office that morning to find Caroline alone at her desk. 'Did you find someone who could help you raise the money?'

'I found someone, yes.'

'Who?'

Caroline pushed aside her typewriter and turned her swivel chair to face the red-haired woman who stood observing her so intently. 'Margery, there's something I must tell you. It's something I wouldn't want you to hear from anyone else.'

Margery pulled out her own chair and sat down. 'This sounds serious.'

'It is.' Caroline passed her tongue nervously over her dry lips. 'I'm going to marry the Lion.'

'Is this some crazy joke?' Margery demanded after a lengthy, incredulous silence.

'I'm not joking, Margery,' Caroline assured her quietly. 'He asked me to marry him, and I agreed.'

'You mean he agreed to pay over the seven thousand rand if you agreed to marry him, is that it?' Margery demanded shrewdly.

'Something like that, yes,' Caroline admitted miserably. 'You see, Margery, we had met before, the Lion and I, but I didn't know at the time who he really was.'

Margery stared at her incredulously. 'You mean you only discovered his identity last week when you were called to his office?'

'Yes,' Caroline nodded, lowering her eyes guiltily for

trying to give the impression that there was something more between Gustav de Leeuw and herself than merely a business agreement.

'It was quite a coincidence, then, that you came to work for his firm?'

'It wasn't a coincidence, Margery,' Caroline admitted honestly despite the hint of sarcasm she had heard in her friend's voice. 'He knew that I needed a job, so he gave me Harold Price's name and told me to contact him.'

'You mean he engineered this position for you.'

Margery's statement was like a slap in the face that awakened her to the truth, and she cringed inwardly with humiliation as she groaned, 'Dear heaven, yes, I realise that now.'

'You shouldn't let it worry you,' Margery advised breezily. 'You'll soon be looking back on this period from your exalted position as Mrs Gustav de Leeuw.'

Being referred to as *Mrs Gustav de Leeuw* at that moment made no impression on Caroline. She sensed a certain animosity in her friend's manner that had the power to hurt, and she said desperately, 'Margery, you don't understand, and I'm afraid I can't explain.'

'What is there to explain? Everything has worked out for the best, hasn't it?' Margery's glance sharpened when Caroline did not reply at once, and she repeated insistently, 'Well, hasn't it?'

'Yes, of course,' Caroline replied lamely, then she raised her eyes pleadingly. 'Margery, I—I hope we can still be friends?'

It seemed for a moment as if Margery had not heard her, then she rose to her feet and held out her hands invitingly towards Caroline with a smile on her lips that was tinged with regret.

'I'm sorry, my dear, if I've been a little bitchy, and naturally we can still be friends.' Her fingers tightened about Caroline's, and her smile was replaced with a look of concern as she added, 'I have a feeling that you're going to need a friend before long.'

Caroline was tempted to question her statement, but the rest of the staff were filtering into the office, and a pile of work awaited her on her desk.

Margery's telephone seemed to go mad that morning with incoming queries, but when it rang again an hour before their lunch break, she extended the receiver towards Caroline and said meaningfully, 'It's for you.'

Caroline's heart leapt into her throat, and her hand trembled when she raised the receiver to her ear and said jerkily, 'Caroline Adams speaking.'

'I'll pick you up outside the entrance to the building at one o'clock sharp,' Gustav de Leeuw's voice sent a little shiver up her spine. 'We have a lot to discuss, and we might as well do so over lunch.'

'Very well,' she managed nervously, and then the line went dead with an abruptness that left her staring stupidly at the instrument in her hand.

'I take it that was someone whose name I shan't mention?' Margery questioned softly.

'Yes,' Caroline replied, dropping the receiver on to its cradle as if it had stung her. 'He wants me to have lunch with him, and he'll pick me up outside the building at one o'clock sharp, he said.'

Margery's eyebrows rose a fraction. 'That information should set a few tongues wagging, and most especially when you're seen together.'

Caroline shrugged with affected casualness, but her stomach seemed to have twisted itself into a knot as she said: 'Everyone will have to know sooner or later.'

When she stepped out into the sunshine an hour later she looked cool and calm in her grey woollen suit and spotless white blouse, but deep down she was a shivering bundle of nerves. A silver Jaguar slid to a halt beside her when she reached the bottom step, and she was all at once embarrassingly conscious of the surprised and speculative glances being directed at her when the man inside the car leaned across to open the door for her.

'Get in,' the Lion ordered tersely, and she obeyed hurriedly in order to escape the small, whispering crowd of people who had gathered on the steps.

Gustav de Leeuw seemed unperturbed by the curious glances directed at them as he set the car in motion, and she almost hated him for it, but her sense of humour returned moments later when she observed the gaping astonishment of the guard posted at the security gate. His hand became suspended in mid-air in the process of saluting, while his jaw dropped several centimetres, and Caroline's tinkling laughter sparked off a glimmer of a smile on the rigid features of the man seated beside her.

'I'm sorry,' she managed at last, stifling her laughter and glancing at her companion selfconsciously and apologetically.

'I would rather have you laughing than looking the way you looked when I picked you up a few minutes ago,' he observed dryly.

'How did I look?' she asked, glancing at him and wishing that her heart would stop behaving so oddly.

'You looked as if you were about to burst into tears,' he said, meeting her startled glance briefly before returning his eyes to the road in time to negotiate a sharp turn to the left. 'Were you on the verge of tears?' he asked unexpectedly when she thought he had forgotten the incident.

'I don't think so,' she laughed nervously. 'I felt self-conscious, though, with so many curious eyes watching me.'

'You'll get used to it,' he said abruptly, 'and you won't have to endure it for very long.'

Caroline did not question his statement, and they travelled in silence the rest of the way to a small restaurant on the foreshore where they were served a crayfish meal with exotic salads. It was delicious, and superbly prepared, but she was too nervous to enjoy it as she would have done under different circumstances.

'I saw Hilton this morning, and that agreement you signed so foolishly has been destroyed,' Gustav told her after they had been served with their coffee. 'He shan't trouble you again,' he added grimly.

Caroline lowered her eyes and murmured inadequately, 'Thank you.'

'That's the first stage of our agreement carried out,' he continued in a businesslike manner. 'The second is our marriage, and I've arranged for it to take place at four o'clock this Saturday afternoon.'

'So soon?' she asked, clasping her hands nervously in her lap beneath the table.

'It will give us a few days to become attuned to each other before Isobel arrives.'

'What about my job?' she tried again, and this time his answer was harsh and abrupt.

'Your services won't be required after Friday.'

Her grey eyes rested thoughtfully for a moment on his hard, unrelenting features, then she said slowly, 'Why do I have the feeling that you've manipulated my life since the day we parted company at your cottage?'

'If you think that then you're absolutely right.' He smiled that twisted smile she had disliked from their first meeting as he continued. 'I had a problem, and I realised soon after meeting you that you would suit me admirably. I saw to it that you were easily accessible, and the moment I heard of your broken engagement I had you investigated more fully to discover your potential. Needless to say, your financial predicament was just the leverage I needed to persuade you into accepting my proposal.' His eyes met hers mockingly across the table. 'Does that shock you?'

Resentment and anger flared within her, but she suppressed it at once and said in a remarkably controlled voice, 'It was supposed to, I'm sure.'

'What I've told you is, however, the truth.'

'I don't doubt it,' she retorted stiffly, then she lost control of her wayward tongue. 'You're arrogant and selfish enough to have done exactly as you said, and more, and if I wasn't so desperate to escape the clutches of Maxwell Hilton, I'd tell you to go to the devil!'

There was a dreadful silence which was disturbed only by the muted voices of the diners in the restaurant, and Caroline could willingly have bitten off her tongue when Gustav leaned his elbows on the table and pinned her to her chair with a cold glance.

'Do you consider that you have the right to criticise me?' he demanded in a dangerously quiet voice.

'No, I suppose not,' she admitted grudgingly, biting down hard on her quivering lip. 'I'm really no better than you are. I'm marrying you for your money, and I despise myself for it.'

His eyebrows rose sharply, then he smiled at her with faint amusement lurking in the depths of his eyes. 'That's one thing I admire about you, Caroline. Your down-to-earth honesty will leave me in no doubt as to what you think of me.'

A tentative smile trembled on her lips. 'What you're really saying is that I'm rude and outspoken.'

'I prefer rudeness and outspokenness to sickly temerity,' he assured her mockingly, 'and I'm convinced that life with you these next two months will certainly not be dull.'

Caroline was not quite sure what he meant by that, but she had a strange feeling that she would not like it if she insisted on an explanation, so she drank the remainder of her coffee in silence, and tried to ignore the vague uneasiness which was beginning to stir within her.

Life for Caroline took a drastic turn towards the unreal. Being seen with Gustav caused a stir among the staff, and she was eyed with a great deal of sly speculation and downright curiosity. When the news of their impending marriage finally leaked out, it was Margery who shielded Caroline by keeping everyone at bay with her sharp tongue.

Shortly after lunch on the Saturday a uniformed delivery man arrived as planned at the boarding house to collect her car, and he handed her a note which she read only when she was alone in her room once more.

'Will call for you at three-thirty sharp,' the note read in characteristic abruptness, and it was signed, 'Gustav.'

His bold handwriting on the white sheet of paper seemed to shake her out of her state of false tranquillity, and she faced the reality of the situation for the first time. This was her wedding day, and within a few short hours she would be Mrs Gustav de Leeuw.

The numbness of fear surged into her limbs, and she sat down heavily on the bed between her two suitcases to stare blankly at the threadbare carpet at her feet. She had the most awful feeling that she was about to do something she would live to regret, but there was nothing she could do to alter the course of events at that late stage. She had walked into it with her eyes wide open, and she would have to see it through to the bitter end.

She glanced at the travelling clock on the bedside table, and leapt to her feet. She had less than two hours in which to bath and change, and if she did not hurry she would never be ready on time.

When the hands of the clock shifted to three-fifteen, she stood staring at herself in the mirror. Her fair silky hair fell softly on to her slim shoulders, and the long-sleeved, ivory-coloured dress she had bought especially for the occasion clung softly to slender curves and flared gently about her shapely legs. Grey eyes, framed with gold-tipped lashes, stared back at her with something close to fear, the nostrils of her small straight nose looked pinched, and the soft pink mouth quivered as though she were hovering on the brink of tears. She was not attractive by the usual standards, but her generous mouth suggested a tenderness and passion she would have denied most fiercely, and her father, from his artistic point of view, had always maintained that she had the most expressive eyes he had ever seen.

Caroline gave none of this a thought while she stared at herself in the mirror. She was more concerned with the fact that she neither looked nor felt like a bride at that moment, and her pale cheeks went a shade paler when there was a sharp tap on her door.

Her fingers fumbled nervously with the zip of her dress which was stuck somewhere between her shoulder blades, but she relinquished her efforts when the knock on her door was repeated, and she opened it with a thudding heart to find Margery standing there.

'Seeing that you're going to have a quiet wedding with no guests to witness the occasion, I thought I'd come along and see if I could be of some assistance to you.' Margery's glance travelled towards the two suitcases stashed neatly at the foot of the bed, then she added with a smile, 'Even if it's just to keep you company.'

'Oh, Margery!' Caroline cried with relief, taking her friend by the hands and literally dragging her inside. 'I'm so glad you've come,' she added breathlessly, closing the door and leaning against it to regain her composure.

Margery eyed her critically. 'Are you nervous?'

'I'm terrified,' Caroline admitted, a note of hysteria in her voice.

'When do you expect the Lion?'

'He should be here any minute now.' At the thought of his impending arrival Caroline stepped away from the door hastily and turned her back towards Margery. 'Would you help me with this, please? I seem to have caught the zip in the material.'

'There, it's done,' said Margery moments later when she had pulled the zip up to the wide collar, then she turned Caroline round to face her. 'You look lovely,' she said at length, her smile embracing Caroline from head to foot.

'Do you really think so?' Caroline asked anxiously, chewing at her bottom lip.

'You couldn't have chosen a better dress to complement your fairness,' Margery assured her emphatically. 'You look like an angel.'

'Oh, Margery . . .'

'For God's sake, don't cry, my dear. You'll ruin your eye make-up, and you've applied it so beautifully.'

Caroline laughed shakily and hugged her friend. 'You're so blessedly practical, Margery, and at this moment I love you for it.'

'My ex-husband despised me for it,' Margery retorted with a grimace. 'He said I didn't have a drop of romantic blood in my veins, and I believe he was right.'

A knock on the door interrupted Caroline's reply, and the haggard-looking face of the manageress peered into the room. 'A Mr de Leeuw is downstairs asking to see you, Miss Adams.'

'Ask him to come up, please,' Caroline said calmly, but her insides began to shake when the woman departed, closing the door behind her.

'Oh, dear,' she muttered nervously, checking her appearance, and thrusting a few last-minute things into her vanity case before she glanced about her wildly. 'Where's my handbag, and my gloves?'

'Here they are,' said Margery, extending them towards her, 'and whatever you do, don't get into a flap.'

'I'll try,' Caroline promised, but when her eyes met Margery's, she whispered urgently, 'Margery, I'm scared.'

'Well, for goodness' sake don't let him see it,' Margery warned in a lowered voice when they heard a step outside the door.

Caroline barely had time to square her shoulders and take a deep, steadying breath before there was a light tap on the door. It opened before she could utter a sound, and the next instant she found herself staring into a pair of catlike eyes that held her glance compellingly. Her heart was beating in her throat, and her trembling fingers tightened on her handbag and gloves as Gustav's eyes travelled systematically down the length of her, then he cast a swift glance about the room.

'Are you ready?' he asked, acknowledging Margery's existence with a brief nod as he stepped into the room and dwarfed it with his size.

'I'm ready,' she managed through stiff lips, then she picked up her vanity case and they followed him silently from the room.

With her suitcases stowed in the boot of the Jaguar, Gustav turned to Margery and addressed her for the first time.

'Are you here with your car, Mrs Doyle?'

'Yes, I am, Mr de Leeuw.'

'Perhaps you would like to come along and give Caroline your moral support?'

Margery looked as if she was about to refuse, but when she met Caroline's pleading glance, she nodded and smiled stiffly. 'I'd love to, thank you.'

'Follow me, then,' Gustav ordered abruptly and, after seeing Caroline into the car, he walked round to the other side and slid in behind the wheel.

It was a cold, wintry afternoon with Table Mountain shrouded in mist, and Caroline wished now that she had thought to leave out her coat. It was warm in Gustav's car, but there had been a chill in the air which had penetrated the warmth of her dress.

When they finally stood outside the small stone church in Constantia, waiting for Margery to catch up to them, Gustav spoke to Caroline again for the first time.

'I regret not engaging a photographer,' he said, glancing down at her from his great height, and making her heart beat faster with what she saw in his eyes. 'You look absolutely charming.'

'A photograph acts as a reminder, and when it's time for our marriage to be dissolved, neither of us may wish to be reminded of this incident in our lives,' she replied without thinking, and his expression hardened until it looked as if his face had been chiselled out of granite.

'You're right, of course,' he said coldly. 'Unpleasant memories should remain forgotten.'

CHAPTER FIVE

In the church, with the clergyman officiating and his wife playing the organ, Gustav and Caroline promised to love and cherish each other for richer, for poorer, in sickness and in health—but it was all lies. The vows they took in the eyes of God were a sham, and Caroline felt slightly sick when they were pronounced man and wife, and told, traditionally, that the groom could kiss the bride.

Strong hands turned her until she looked a long way up into those hard, chiselled features, and if she had expected to see some sign of emotion there, then she was mistaken. Gustav's eyes were cold, and so were his lips when they brushed against hers, but her heart seemed not to know the difference, for it pounded madly against her ribs.

'*Smile*, for heaven's sake!' Margery whispered urgently when she had the opportunity to offer her congratulations, and Caroline obliged even though she felt more like bursting into tears.

'I'm so glad that you were here,' she said with a ring of deep sincerity in her lowered voice, and Margery leaned forward to kiss her on the cheek.

'You know my address. If you ever need me, just call.'

Gustav's approach ended their conversation, and when they stepped out of the church a few minutes later, the sun burst through the clouds to shed a warm glow over the earth. Whether it was a good or a bad omen, Caroline did not know. The only thing she was sure of at that moment was that her nerves had become so knotted that she was afraid they might never become unravelled again.

'This was not exactly the kind of wedding you visualised for yourself, was it?' Gustav remarked in his usual cynical manner when, at last, they drove away from the church.

'I never imagined that I would have an elaborate wedding, if that's what you mean, but I did imagine I would be married under different circumstances.'

'You still have that to look forward to. If all goes well, you'll be free in less than three months, then you can wipe this incident from your memory.'

Stung by his remark for some inexplicable reason, she said angrily, 'I can't wait to do that.'

He glanced at her briefly and smiled that twisted smile. 'Your Dennis might even set aside his pompous attitude and consider taking you back.'

'He might,' she retorted, knowing in her heart that she would never change her mind about Dennis even if he came back to her on bended knees.

'That would make you happy, wouldn't it?' he asked mockingly.

'It would,' she snapped untruthfully.

'Will you invite me to your wedding?' he questioned her, and at the sound of her faint gasp he glanced at her briefly once again with raised eyebrows. 'I could take the place of your father,' he explained caustically.

'You're not that old,' she stated flatly.

'I'm thirty-nine,' he laughed shortly, 'and to a child like yourself that must sound as if I'm in my dotage.'

Caroline stared at him contemplatively for a moment, then she asked, 'Do you want me to think of you as my father?'

'I'm damned if I do!' he exploded, and she was forced to hide her smile of amusement by turning her head away to look out of the window.

They were approaching his home when she glanced at him frowningly, and asked: 'Don't you ever want a real marriage with children to carry on your name?'

'The answer is "no" to both,' he replied harshly, swinging the car to the right to drive through the stone gateposts of La Roche and up the circular driveway towards the house. 'I become too easily bored with women, and I can't think of anything I want less than a screaming little brat about the place.'

Caroline's eyes widened with shock, and a silence settled between them that was only broken when he placed her suitcases on the carpeted floor in the hall and turned to face the servant woman who approached them.

'Tilly will show you up to your room if you'd like to freshen up, and I suggest that you bring a coat or something warm down with you,' he instructed after making the necessary introductions, but when he met Caroline's questioning glance, he added abruptly, 'We're dining out tonight.'

He turned and strode into the living-room, leaving Caroline to follow Tilly up the carpeted stairs and along a passage towards the east side of the house. She eventually put down the suitcases to open one of the numerous doors, and stood aside respectfully for Caroline to precede her into the room.

A solid oak four-poster bed dominated the large room, and Caroline's frightened glance registered very little else except that the gold curtains at the window matched the carpet and the bedspread.

'I'll unpack for you while you're out this evening,

madam,' Tilly told her as she placed the suitcases neatly on the floor at the foot of the bed.

'That won't be necessary, Tilly,' Caroline said quickly, turning to smile a little nervously at the black woman, who stood observing her a little curiously. 'I wouldn't like to trouble you to that extent.'

'It will be no trouble, madam,' Tilly assured her brightly. 'Just leave everything to me.'

Tilly was gone before she could reply, but as Caroline altered her position slightly, she found herself staring at her own image in the mirror of the oak dressing-table. Good heavens! she thought, staring at herself a little more closely. Was that frightened-looking individual herself? It was no wonder that Tilly observed her with such curiosity, she decided, making an effort to pull herself together as she explored her immediate surroundings.

A spacious dressing-room adjoined the bedroom, and beyond that she found the bathroom with every modern convenience one could imagine. She washed her hands and touched up her make-up, pausing only for a moment to stare at the unfamiliar gold band on her finger before she hurriedly pulled her camelhair coat out of her suitcase and went downstairs to join Gustav.

He emerged from the depths of the wing-backed chair beside the fireplace, and poured her a glass of wine when she entered the living-room. With the delicate, long-stemmed glass between her fingers, she moved closer to the warmth of the fire, and seated herself on the chair facing Gustav's. A silence seemed to descend on the house which was disturbed only by the ticking of the grandfather clock in the hall, and the crackling of the log fire. She raised her glass to her lips, and her eyes suddenly met those of the man seated opposite her.

Caroline's heart missed a beat as she sipped at her wine and tried to look away, but the strange, glittering quality of his eyes held hers captive. A warmth flowed through her veins which she could not attribute entirely to the wine, and her pulse rate quickened in the way it had done that night in his cottage when he had kissed her. She did not want to recall those moments when she had been awakened to emotions she had not thought she possessed, but deep down inside her there was an unfamiliar yearning to feel the strength of his arms about her once again. It frightened her to think that this man she had married a little more than an hour ago could make her feel this way, and, wrenching her eyes from his, she questioned him about something which she had found a little confusing.

'If this house was left to your stepmother, why has she been living in Namibia since your father's death?'

She thought for a moment that he was not going to answer her, then his mouth twisted into a mirthless smile. 'Isobel and I don't get on very well. We never have, and we never will. She wanted me out of the way, but my father's will fortunately stipulated that this remains my home for as long as I wish, so she moved out to her family in Namibia in preference to remaining here under my watchful eyes, and if she ever decides to sell the house, then she will have to give me first option.'

'Do you have an idea that she might want to sell it?'

'Not at the moment, no,' he said, his mouth twisting again into a semblance of a smile, 'but when the time is right I shall make her an offer she won't be able to refuse.'

Caroline drained her glass while she considered this, then she said tentatively, 'You've obviously formed some plan of action in your mind.'

'I have, yes,' he answered abruptly, 'but I shall play it largely by ear.' He rose to his feet then, and she sensed an underlying impatience as he looked down at her from his autocratic height. 'Shall we go?'

She nodded, and with his hand beneath her elbow, they walked out of the house to where he had left the Jaguar parked in the driveway.

On this occasion he took her to a restaurant on the foreshore where they could dine and dance, or simply sit and watch the cabaret while they enjoyed their *à la carte* meal. Caroline had heard of places such as this, but she had never imagined anything so luxurious, and she looked about her with interest while Gustav ordered their meal and asked for a bottle of champagne to be brought to their table.

Concealed lighting threw a soft glow over the candlelit tables set with gleaming silver on spotless white linen, and couples danced in tune to music supplied by a fashionable orchestra, while others dined amid laughter and the murmur of voices.

A glass of bubbling champagne settled the slight flutter at the pit of Caroline's stomach, and somehow she began to relax in Gustav's company. He kept up a flow of light, entertaining conversation while they dined, and Caroline actually found herself giggling at some of the outrageous remarks he passed about some of their fellow diners. The cabaret show interrupted their conversation from time to time, and it did so again at that moment when half a dozen girls pranced on to the stage to indulge in a wild, gyrating dance that made Caroline blush at the suggestiveness of their movements. She glanced quickly at Gustav, but that was a mistake, for her colour deepened when she met his mocking glance resting so intently on her person. She averted her eyes hastily, but she was eventually so aware of the intensity of his gaze that she felt she had been stripped as naked as those scantily clad girls on the stage. Her heart seemed to be hammering somewhere in her throat, choking off her breath, but it fortunately returned to normality when Gustav turned slightly in his chair to applaud the girls as they disappeared behind the blue velvet curtains.

When he turned back to face her, she hastily diverted the conversation away from her by asking, 'What do you think your stepmother will do when she discovers that you're married?'

'That's difficult to say,' he shrugged slightly. 'She's a very clever woman, and she won't give up easily.'

'She sounds a little frightening.'

His expression hardened visibly. 'Whatever you do, don't be intimidated by her. You have enough spark in your character to give back as much as you receive, and I shall be relying on you.'

Whatever Caroline had imagined before, she realised now that this was no game. It was of great importance to Gustav to maintain control of the business his father had started before him, and she would have to play her part in this charade with care.

'I hope I shan't fail you,' she said eventually, her wide, grey glance meeting his levelly.

'I know you won't,' he replied with a tight smile curving his mouth, then, as the orchestra resumed its playing, he rose to his feet and held out his hand towards her. 'Shall we dance?'

With her small hand almost disappearing in his clasp, he led her on to the dance floor, and then his arm was about her waist, holding her firmly against him as they moved around the floor in time to the music.

Caroline was fond of dancing, but never before had

her steps matched her partner's so perfectly, and never before had she experienced such a singing joy at the impersonal touch of a man's body against her own. The music was slow and sentimental, and she had the oddest sensation that she was drifting on a cloud somewhere between heaven, and a strange new delight. Her nervousness disappeared, and Gustav's arm tightened about her at once when he felt her relax against him. She looked up into his light, unfathomable eyes, and at the lips so close to her own as he bent his head towards her, then the most peculiar thing happened to her. Her heart seemed to swell with an emotion so strong that she trembled with the force of it and, afraid of what he might see in her eyes, she buried her face against his broad shoulder.

She was going slightly crazy, or perhaps the champagne and the music had affected her usual good sense, but no matter what excuse she tried to find for her deranged condition, she could not deny to herself that she was falling in love with a man who had made it potently clear from the start that she would not be needed once he had achieved his goal.

She tried not to think of it; tried to tell herself that it had not happened, but as they danced the evening away it became increasingly difficult to think of anything else. One thing she realised, however, was that she would have to make use of every available means to hide her feelings. Whatever happened, Gustav must never know that she had been silly enough to lay her heart at his feet.

He was silent in the car when they drove back to La Roche late that night, but Caroline was too busy trying to sort her emotions into their proper place to take much notice. He let them into the house with his own key and, with his hand beneath her elbow, accompanied her upstairs to her room, but, contrary to what she had expected, he followed her in and closed the door behind him.

Without a word he removed his jacket and tie and flung them on to the chair in the corner, then he proceeded to unbutton his white, silk shirt, exposing his tanned, hair-roughened chest bit by bit before her horrified eyes.

'What are you doing?' she demanded at last when she managed to find her voice, but it sounded faint and jerky to her ears.

'I'm getting undressed, as you can see,' he said, tugging his shirt out of his pants.

'But you can't!' she cried in a choked voice. 'Not here!'

'My dear child, we're married, and this also happens to be my bedroom,' he mocked her as he discarded his shirt.

She stared hypnotically at his muscled arms and chest, and swallowed convulsively. 'You mean you intend sleeping here?'

With his hands resting on his hips he glanced beyond her and back again into her frightened eyes. 'That bed is big enough for two.'

'You're no better than Maxwell Hilton! In fact, you're worse!' she accused hoarsely, her colour coming and going. 'He at least made it quite clear what he wanted.'

'There is a difference, if you would care to think about it,' he contradicted mockingly. 'He offered to set you up as his mistress, but I married you.'

'You made me believe that our marriage would be a business arrangement,' she retorted angrily.

'And so it is,' he murmured, sliding his glance up and down the length of her in a way that made her skin feel heated. 'I see no reason, however, why we shouldn't enjoy each other while our marriage lasts.'

Caroline stared at him in stupefied silence, then panic dictated her actions and she brushed past him, heading towards the door. 'I'm leaving!'

His fingers snaked about her wrist in a vicelike grip before she had gone four paces, and she was swung round roughly to face him.

'Cut out the dramatics and listen to reason,' he ordered harshly, looking down into her blazing eyes. 'We have to share the same room as well as the same bed if we're to convince Isobel that we're actually married—and believe me, she'll need convincing that this marriage was not organised to cheat her son Russell out of an inheritance which is rightfully mine.' His expression hardened perceptibly. 'You owe it to me, remember?'

A wave of helplessness surged through her as she looked up into those cold eyes boring down into her, and she found nothing there to lighten her heart at that moment. 'I think I'm beginning to dislike you intensely.'

'I have a feeling that you'll dislike me even more by the time our marriage is terminated,' he said in a clipped voice, then he released his grip on her wrist and turned his back on her in a dismissive manner. 'You can use the bathroom first,' he added over his shoulder.

Caroline slipped her coat off her shoulders and walked through into the dressing-room on unsteady legs, closing the door firmly behind her. In the pinewood cupboards with the slatted doors she found Gustav's clothes as well as her own, and suddenly the situation developed nightmare qualities that made the blood run cold in her veins.

She bathed quickly and slipped into her lacy nightdress before putting on her wide-sleeved silk robe which she had bought in one of her rare extravagant moods and, pushing her feet into soft mules, she checked that she had left the bathroom in order. At the door leading into the bedroom she paused nervously. She had never appeared before any man, except her father, in her night attire, and the thought of Gustav seeing her dressed this way filled her with intense shyness. To all intents and purposes he was her husband, the man she would have to share the same bed with in order to make their marriage seem convincing, but heaven only knew how she was going to endure what still lay ahead of her. Within the space of hours she had discovered that she could love and despise him with equal intensity, and it frightened her to think that she was capable of two such terrifyingly strong emotions.

She stared hard at the door and, knowing that she could no longer delay entering their bedroom, she squared her shoulders and turned the handle. Gustav was reclining in a chair with his eyes closed and a cigar smouldering between his fingers. He had discarded his shoes and socks, but he was still wearing his pants, she noticed, and as she ventured farther into the room he opened his eyes unexpectedly, and his gaze met hers. Her cheeks grew warm, but when his glance travelled with a lazy sensuality down the length of her, she felt herself go rigid with fear and embarrassment.

She turned away jerkily towards the dressing-table where Tilly had set out a few of her personal things and, picking up her brush, began to brush her hair with quick, firm strokes. She was trying desperately to look calm and unmoved by Gustav's disturbing presence, but her heart leapt uncomfortably when she glanced into the mirror and saw him rise from his chair. Their eyes met and held for one paralysing instant, then he turned and disappeared into the dressing-room, closing the door behind him.

Caroline felt herself sag with relief and, putting down her brush, she took off her robe and climbed into bed. Perhaps, by some stroke of luck, she would be asleep when he returned and, pulling the blankets up to beneath her chin, she switched off the light on her side of the bed and turned on to her side so that her back would be to Gustav.

Sleep, however, evaded her. She was conscious of the shower being turned on, and of his tuneless whistle which she had heard once before when she had slept in his cottage, but most of all she was conscious of a growing tension that held her mercilessly in its grip. She was convinced that she would never sleep that night, not with Gustav sharing the same bed with her, and she turned her ashen face into the pillow, wishing herself anywhere but there at that moment.

The shower was eventually turned off, but the tuneless whistling continued for a time until that, too, ceased abruptly, plunging the suite into a silence which she found nerve-shattering. She lay perfectly still, almost holding her breath, then the dressing-room door opened, and her body went rigid. She closed her eyes tightly, pretending to be asleep as she sensed Gustav approaching the bed, then her heart was beating so hard and fast that she was certain he must hear it. She waited, paralysed with a mixture of shyness and fear, then she felt him lower himself on to the bed beside her, and switch off the light to plunge the room into darkness.

'Goodnight, Caroline,' he said unexpectedly, startling

her with the knowledge that she had not succeeded in fooling him, and leaving her no alternative but to reciprocate.

'Goodnight,' she whispered unsteadily, grateful that the darkness hid the flush that stole into her cheeks.

She tried to ignore the fact that Gustav was lying so close to her that one careless movement might result in their bodies touching, but the harder she tried, the worse it became, until some of her tension must have been relayed to him.

'For God's sake, Caroline, relax!' he ordered harshly, switching on the light and turning her roughly over on to her back so that she was forced to look up into his granite-hard face.

'I—I've never slept with a man before,' she explained miserably.

'There always has to be a first time with everything in one's life.'

His eyes glittered mockingly down into hers, and she became alarmingly aware of his tantalising masculine scent, the wide expanse of his shoulders casting a shadow over her, and the touch of his hand against her skin as it travelled from her shoulder to her throat. She was totally vulnerable at that moment and, knowing this, she resorted to anger.

'I think you're absolutely without sympathy or understanding!'

His mouth tightened ominously, as did the fingers about her throat. 'I'm not a sex maniac, if that's what you're afraid of, and I don't intend pouncing on a child like yourself merely to satisfy my sexual appetite.'

'I'm not a child!' she argued, her colour deepening.

'No, by heaven, you're not,' he agreed thickly, sliding his hand deliberately and without tenderness beneath the lacy neckline of her nightdress to clasp her breast.

She gasped at the unexpectedness of it, but his mouth came down on to hers with a stifling pressure, draining her of the desire to resist, and leaving only that strange excitement which she had encountered once before. A warmth flowed through her, filling her with an aching need she did not quite understand, but when she trembled with the force of it, he released her and rolled over on to his side of the bed.

'Go to sleep,' he ordered harshly, switching off the light. 'I shan't trouble you.'

Caroline lay staring into the darkness for a long time, trying to cope with her thudding heart, and a deep-seated disappointment as if she had been bereft of something she could not even begin to understand. Gustav's deep, even breathing finally told her that he was asleep, and only then did the tension ease from her body. Her eyelids drooped and, at last, she slept.

She had no idea how long she slept, but she awoke with a start when a heavy weight was flung across her waist. It took her several seconds to realise that it was Gustav's arm, and then she was wide awake to the warmth of his body against her own. She tried to shift out from under his arm, but he grunted something unintelligible and merely tightened his hold.

Caroline was at a loss as to what she should do, but when his hand slid down along her thigh, she wriggled against him in a frantic effort to escape, and regardless as to whether she awakened him.

His hand tightened on her thigh, and by the sound of his breathing she knew that he was no longer asleep, but instead of releasing her, he drew her closer until her small softness was moulded to the hard contours of his body.

'My God, this is impossible,' he groaned into her ear, then his mouth found hers in the darkness with a sensuality that sent a shock of sensations storming through her.

There had been no time to utter a protest, and no time to escape the strength of those muscled arms imprisoning her, but as he plundered the sweetness of her soft lips she knew only the desire that he should never let her go.

Her fingers uncurled themselves against his hair-roughened chest and moved upwards of their own volition to grip his smooth, hard shoulders, but she was unprepared for the way he reacted upon her innocent and unknowing caress. He shuddered against her, unleashing the passion he had kept under such tight control, then his lips and hands were all over her body, seeking and finding unheard-of intimacies that would have made her blush profusely under saner circumstances.

She was losing control of her emotions, and the pleasurable sensations that rippled through her body were as alien to her as the strange need that raced through her veins like heated liquid. She was afraid, too; afraid of where this was leading to, and afraid of her own inability to resist, but when Gustav scooped her close to his heated body with a purposeful intent not even she could mistake, her sanity returned, and fear left her cold and devoid of the emotions he had aroused moments before.

'Gustav, no!' she pleaded frantically, her hands flat against his hard chest, and the muscles in her arms aching with the effort to thrust him away, but his hard thigh was between her own, and his weight was forcing her deeper into the softness of the bed.

'It's too late,' he growled thickly against her throat, and then she knew what it was to be completely possessed by a man.

Later, when he lay sleeping beside her, she was still trying to stop the flow of tears that continued to dampen her pillow. She felt cold and disillusioned, and it was a long time before she was calm enough to think of sleeping, but when the dawn light filtered into the room she was still awake, and labouring under an incredible weariness.

Gustav was still asleep, and he was lying on his back with one arm flung above his head. He looked younger, somehow, with his features softened in sleep, but even as she watched him he stirred, and his features became set once again into its familiar harsh pattern.

She sat up quickly and swung her legs off the bed, but she was stopped in the process of reaching for her robe.

'Caroline . . .'

She glanced down at the hand gripping her arm, and her throat tightened with fear. 'Let me go!'

He released her at once, but a harshness had crept into his voice when he said: 'Very few women enjoy it the first time, and you were no exception. Next time——'

'There won't be a next time!' she interrupted heatedly, her cheeks flaring as she pulled on her robe and tightened the belt about her waist.

'Don't be too sure of that,' his mocking rejoinder followed her into the dressing-room, and at that moment she came close once more to hating him.

Caroline could not face Gustav that morning, not after what had occurred between them during the dark

hours of the night, and she was infinitely relieved when
he excused himself after breakfast and disappeared
into what she presumed to be his study. It gave her the
opportunity to acquaint herself with the house, and she
spent more than an hour exploring the many rooms,
some of which had dust covers draped over the priceless
antique furniture. Family portraits lined the walls of the
large dining hall, but one portrait in particular drew her
attention. It had to be a portrait of Gustav's father, for
the strong, rugged features were the same, while those
incredibly light eyes possessed that piercing quality that
seemed to delve without permission into the most secret
recesses of one's soul. Provision had been made for a
portrait to hang alongside that of Gustav's father, but
the space was conspicuously empty. A portrait had hung
there once, judging by the faint discoloration on the
whitewashed wall, but it had been removed for some
reason, and Caroline could not help wondering whose
portrait it had been, and why it should have been taken
down.

It was with this puzzling thought in mind that she
paused in front of yet another door, and tried the
handle. It was locked.

'You'll need a key to go in there, but I wouldn't
advise it.'

She swung round sharply to face the man who had
come up behind her so silently, and she found herself
trapped between the door and those coldly mocking eyes
that made her nerve-ends quiver protestingly.

'Why wouldn't you advise it?' she asked, not quite
succeeding in her attempt to sound casual.

'This used to be the old wine-cellar,' he explained in a
clipped voice. 'It's been stripped of almost everything
relating to those fruitful years when wine flowed from

the caskets to tease the palates of the master and his guests. These days the cellar is nothing but a store-room to house those unwanted objects.'

'You sound as if you object to the cellar being used as a store-room.'

'I believe in preservation, not destruction, but many things were considered not worth preserving after Isobel took charge of this house.'

His features took on that familiar brooding expression, and she broke the threatening silence by saying tentatively, 'I'd still like to see the cellar, if I may.'

His eyes seemed to focus on her once more, and that gleam of mockery was there once again as he reached up to remove the key from the ledge above the door. 'If you're not allergic to cobwebs and dust, then I'll take you down.'

He inserted the key in the lock and moments later the door swung open on creaking hinges. Caroline stared down into the inky blackness of the cellar, and wished suddenly that she had not been so insistent in wanting to see what lay beyond that door as she felt herself shiver inwardly.

CHAPTER SIX

GUSTAV snapped on the light, and the cellar lost a great deal of its scariness, then he took her arm and guided her down the steep, narrow steps which seemed to lead down into the bowels of the earth where the musty smell was at first almost overpowering.

Evidence of it having been a wine-cellar was everywhere to be seen. Two wine-casks still remained in what appeared to be their original positions, while at the farthest end of the cellar a wine-press and an old-fashioned bottling machine stood forgotten under layers of dust. What interesting and exciting museum pieces they would have made, Caroline could not help thinking.

'Do old houses interest you?' Gustav interrupted her thoughts with a note of amusement in his voice, but his amusement bordered on a mockery that very nearly succeeded in angering her.

'Old houses interest me very much,' she stated adamantly, casting her glance over the array of boxes, old travelling trunks, and discarded furniture. 'They have so much character.'

'Old houses have their ghosts, too.'

Caroline glanced up at Gustav in the dim light with a degree of uncertainty in her eyes. 'You're teasing me, surely?'

His mouth twitched slightly. 'Do you believe in ghosts?'

'I've never encountered one.' She slanted another

questioning glance up at him. 'Have you?'

'The servants complained that on certain nights they heard someone wailing down here in the cellar. I came down here on one such a night and discovered that when the wind blows in a certain direction it enters through a crack in the wall and produces a sound which could be mistaken for someone crying out in a mournful manner.' His mocking smile deepened. 'Does that answer your question?'

'You believe there's a simple explanation for everything?' she asked, unable to suppress the little shiver that raced through her.

'There usually is,' he answered abruptly, drawing himself up to his full height. 'Have you seen enough?'

'I think so,' she murmured slowly, but when she turned she glimpsed an object which stood propped up against a towering assortment of boxes in the corner.

Without asking his permission she climbed over several dusty objects in her path to reach what appeared to be a painting. It stood with its face turned away from the light and, showing a total disregard for the layer of dust which covered the gilt frame, Caroline turned it round and stood back a fraction to admire the dust-covered portrait of a fair-haired, fair-skinned woman with her slender figure resplendent in white lace and glittering jewels. There was something familiar about the broad forehead and the shape of the long-lashed eyes, but Caroline could not quite place it at that moment.

'My father had that portrait painted of my mother soon after their marriage.'

The sound of Gustav's voice directly behind her startled her into saying, 'Why it is gathering dust down here in the cellar?'

'Isobel was a jealous, possessive wife, and she ordered

the portrait to be removed from its place in the dining hall,' Gustav explained bluntly.

'Surely your father had a say in the matter?'

'My father was too busy making money to care eventually what went on in his home,' came the harsh reply, and she flinched inwardly at the bitterness she detected there.

'May I clean up the portrait and put it back where it belongs?'

'If you like,' he said after a slight pause, his face taut and cynical. 'It might be interesting to watch Isobel's reaction when she notices it.'

'It wasn't Isobel I was thinking of when I suggested it,' she retorted angrily, but she could have bitten off her tongue the next moment when she observed that hateful gleam of mockery in his light eyes.

'Did you think it would please me to see my mother's portrait hanging in its rightful place?'

He was right, of course. She *had* thought briefly that it would please him, but she could never let him know that she had been foolish enough to think along those lines. As a matter of fact, he had had plenty of time to rescue the portrait from its dusty grave, but she still had plenty of time to discover why he had not bothered to do so.

'It's a terrible waste to leave such a work of art to rot in the cellar,' she explained at last, grasping at the first thought that came to mind, and his expression became curiously shuttered.

'I agree with you.'

To Caroline's surprise Gustav not only helped her to carry the portrait from the cellar, but he also helped her rid it of the dust and cobwebs it had gathered over the years, and she was proud of their efforts when it finally hung against the wall alongside the portrait of his father in the dining hall.

'Was she a small woman?' she ventured to ask as she admired those slender hands clasped together so lightly amidst the lacy folds of the dress.

'Small and fair, yes,' Gustav acknowledged, his critical glance raking Caroline from the top of her fair head down to her knee-high boots. 'Something like yourself, I believe,' he added, taking in the flush that stained her cheeks.

'You must take after your father,' she remarked, trying to ignore the effect this man was having on her. 'You look very much like him.'

'My father was a hard man to please, but he met his match in Isobel. She was equally hard and ruthless when it came to getting what she wanted.'

She digested this information carefully, then she asked: 'What makes you think that she won't succeed this time in getting what she wants?'

'This time she has *me* to deal with, and there's no way she can get around the fact that I've complied with the stipulations in the will.' She felt his eyes on her, willing her to look up at him, but she refused to give in to the silent command as she fastened her gaze on the portrait she had rescued from the cellar, and only the tiny pulse beating furiously at the base of her throat gave some indication of her disturbed emotions when he added with an undercurrent of deliberate sensuality in his voice, 'I have a wife, don't I, in every sense of the word?'

A choking sensation rose in her throat, making her swallow convulsively as she turned away from him, then she said thickly, 'I think I'd like to go for a walk.'

'I have a better idea.' Strong fingers gripped her wrist, and halted her in her effort to escape, but she still refused to look at him. 'We'll take a drive round the peninsula and stop somewhere for lunch.'

She was given no time to offer a protest and, wrapped

up warmly in the only coat she possessed, she found herself seated beside him in his silver Jaguar while he drove out towards Simonstown on the road that bordered False Bay. Caroline had been on this road many times before, but with Gustav it was a totally new experience which made her feel as if she were seeing it all for the very first time. He knew the history of every hamlet and village like the back of his hand, and he held her rapt attention with incidents she had never heard of before. At Kalk Bay, for instance, he paused to inform her that the Kalk (chalk) in the name referred to the lime-kilns which had been set up there in the seventeenth century, but Kalk Bay, Caroline knew, was now nothing more than a small fishing village.

Beyond Partridge Point the road turned north-west along the Rooihoogte and Bonteberg mountains to Slangkoppunt (Snake Head Point), then east again for some five kilometres before turning north along the Chapman's Peak drive towards Hout Bay where they stopped at a restaurant for lunch.

Caroline was more conscious of the man seated opposite her than of the lobster dish she had ordered, and once, when his knee brushed against hers accidentally beneath the table, she became aware of a tingling sensation quivering along her nervous system. Gustav had been acting the perfect host, and she felt herself slipping under the spell of his magnetism until she was convinced that she had been mesmerised.

The sea had never been bluer, nor the sun so bright, she thought when they continued their drive northwards along the west coast of the peninsula, and by the time they reached the Kirstenbosch Gardens she was responding to every nuance in his voice like someone enslaved. They indulged in a slow walk along one of the many paths amidst the assortment of indigenous trees and shrubs, few of which flowered at that time of the year, but it did not seem to matter. It was a warm afternoon filled with birdsong and the wild smell of the eucalyptus trees, and Caroline came close to savouring a peculiar type of contentment.

They passed the oval-shaped bath where Lady Anne Barnard had reputedly bathed daily during her husband's reign as Colonial Secretary from 1797 to 1802, and it was then that something flew into Caroline's hair to disturb her tranquillity.

'Stand still,' Gustav ordered when he noticed her distress. 'You have a beetle in your hair.'

He stood so close to her that the male scent of him invaded her nostrils and stirred her senses, while his fingers seemed to linger disturbingly in the silken strands of her hair. For one mad moment she wanted to press closer to him, but she suppressed the desire to do so, and clenched her hands at her sides to prevent herself from touching him.

The beetle was flicked from her hair and, almost as if he sensed the battle for sanity going on inside her, he caught her quivering chin between his fingers and raised her face to this. She caught a brief glimpse of those glittering, catlike eyes, then his lips descended on hers, softly at first, and then with an insistent pressure that left no room for thought. She could have avoided that kiss, and even now she could have stepped away from him. There was nothing to prevent her from doing so except the weakness that had assailed her limbs, and which held her captive as surely as if his arms had imprisoned her against him.

When Gustav finally raised his head she felt as intoxicated as if she had consumed too much wine with her lunch, and she was not quite certain of anything except the touch of his hand on her arm as he guided her back along the path to where he had parked his car.

On the drive back to La Roche her sanity returned and, sensing her withdrawal, he placed a seemingly casual hand on her thigh, but his touch had the desired effect, and she was drawn once again into that cocoon of sensual awareness which he had spun so skilfully about her.

At La Roche his arm went about her, his hand firm and warm against her waist, when they entered the house, crossed the hall, and climbed the many steps up to their bedroom. Caroline knew what was about to happen when he closed the door behind him and drew her into his arms, but she felt incapable of doing anything about altering the course of events.

The touch of his lips and hands was compelling, and aroused her until, drugged with desire, she allowed him to undress her and lower her on to the bed. Somehow, without her being aware of it, he had divested himself of his own clothes, and when he gathered her against the muscled hardness of his male body she quivered like a helpless butterfly beneath his hands. His caresses were slow, persistent and sensual, awakening a flame within her which refused to be doused. She tried to speak, to protest at the intimacies he sought, but not a sound passed her lips while her body, seemingly with a mind of its own, arched towards his, and it was an unspoken invitation which he did not ignore. She expected pain, but experienced only a pleasure that intensified until she was no longer in control of what she was doing.

Gustav's skin was moist, the muscles in his back rippling with tautness as she slid her hands upwards to draw his head down to hers until their lips met once more in a searing kiss. She could no longer think, only feel, and neither did she care what he thought of her as she locked her arms about his neck and buried her face against him. Something was happening to her; something so totally alien that every nerve and sinew in her body became centred on this new kind of tension which was now rapidly reaching the stage where she was beginning to find it intolerable.

'Gustav! Oh, Gustav, please!' she heard herself begging a little huskily, then her voice changed to a cry of delight as the tension snapped within her and the most exquisite sensations rippled through her body.

Later, when sanity returned, she escaped from his arms and fled into the bathroom where wave after wave of shame engulfed her. She had become a stranger to herself, but not entirely a mystery. She loved Gustav; loved him in a way she had never imagined possible, but not once, not by word or gesture, had he given the slightest indication that he cared for her, and the most distressing part of it all was that she knew he never would.

Caroline bathed and dressed for dinner, and when Gustav emerged from the shower she tried to ignore the tanned, muscular attraction of his body which was clothed only in a towel draped rather carelessly about his lean hips. He came up behind her, and his eyes met her mutinous grey glance in the dressing-table mirror.

'It's not the end of the world, you know,' he mocked her. 'For you it's only the beginning.'

An angry retort rose to her lips, but it died swiftly as she faced the terrifying truth. Her world would end the day Gustav no longer needed her. It was a stunning and rather frightening thought, and one that made her walk rather blindly from his presence.

Gustav was oddly silent throughout dinner that evening, and later, when they sat in front of the living-room fire, he smoked a pipe instead of the cigar she was fast becoming accustomed to seeing clenched between his teeth. His face wore that brooding expression she had noticed for the first time when she had spent those two nights with him in his cottage, but on this occasion she sensed a sadness in him which seemed strangely out of place in this derisive, normally harsh man.

It had to be her imagination, she decided, and as her thoughts turned to the immediate future, she asked: 'What will you expect of me when Isobel and her family arrive?'

'I shall expect you to behave as any loyal wife would behave when her husband's future is threatened.' There was a warning note in his deep, harsh voice which she could not miss. 'Be prepared for anything, from Isobel as well as Russell. Isobel is the force behind it all, while Russell merely does as he's told.'

'He sounds like a weakling,' Caroline observed loudly without actually intending to, and Gustav's eyebrows rose sharply.

'I wouldn't say that, but Isobel is very clever, and very dominating.'

She slanted a curious glance at him. 'Did she dominate you when you were a child?'

'She tried.'

'But she didn't succeed,' she stated quietly when she noticed the smirk on his face.

'Obviously not,' he mocked. 'I wouldn't be what I am today if she had succeeded.'

She looked away from the probing intensity of his eyes and wondered just how she was going to cope with the future.

With an uncanny knack of being able to sense her thoughts, Gustav said: 'You haven't an easy task ahead of you, and you may yet find yourself wishing that you'd accepted Maxwell Hilton's proposition instead of mine.'

'Oh, no! Never! I——' She halted confusedly and

blushed deeply at the only interpretation he could place on her outburst and, rising quickly on to unsteady legs, she added jerkily, 'I think I'll go upstairs, if you don't mind.'

'Caroline!' His voice stopped her before she reached the door, and strong hands gripped her shoulders, making her realise that he had moved with incredible silence and speed. The smell of tobacco mingled with his masculine cologne to form a tantalising combination which stirred her senses, and the touch of that sensual, seeking mouth against her throat and ear was almost her undoing. 'Can it be,' he demanded in a soft, mocking voice, 'that you've decided you prefer my lovemaking to what you might have suffered at the hands of Hilton?'

Her colour deepened, and her errant heart beat out a mad tattoo against her ribs, but she resorted to anger as her only defence.

'I think you're hateful!' she spat out the words. 'Last night should never have happened, and I'm ashamed of the way I behaved this afternoon.'

She was propelled round to face him and, against her will, her stormy eyes met his, but she lowered her lashes instantly before the compelling mastery of his gaze.

'I don't regret for one moment making love to you last night, and this afternoon you wanted me as much as I wanted you.'

'Let me go!' she cried, pummelling his hard chest with her clenched fists in an effort to vent her anger and humiliation on him. 'I hate you to touch me!'

He caught her wrists neatly and twisted them behind her back, imprisoning her against him so that she could not help but be aware of every hard line of his body against her own.

'Your lips say one thing, but your eyes speak differently,' he chided her mockingly. 'I wonder which I should believe?'

'I hate you!' she hissed, straining against the arms that held her.

'Hate is a very positive emotion, and I think I like it. The more you hate me, my dear Caroline, the more I find that I want you.'

His cynical mouth descended on hers with a practised sensuality and, despite herself, she melted against him and was lost for a moment in the rapture only he could create for her. When her sanity returned, she resumed her struggles, but Gustav lifted her in his arms as if she weighed nothing more than a child, then he carried her from the living-room. As he ascended the stairs his laughter mocked her puny efforts to escape the steel trap of his arms, and tears of frustration finally glittered on her gold-tipped lashes when he entered their bedroom and kicked the door shut behind him.

'You little wildcat!' he snarled, setting her on her feet when he narrowly escaped his cheek being raked by her fingernails. 'I'll tame you yet,' he warned thickly, gripping her wrists and twisting her arms until she cried out in agony. 'And I'll hurt you a damn sight more if you ever try that again!'

Her ceaseless struggles seemed to awaken an angry passion within him, and there was no gentleness in the way he ripped her clothes from her shivering body before discarding his own. There was no escape, either, from the violating intimacy of his hands, but instead of dampening her emotions, his touch seemed to inflame her with a desire that seared through her veins in the most intoxicating manner, and she surrendered finally with an incoherent little cry to the demands he was making on her.

It had been like riding the crest of a stormy wave, she

recalled afterwards as she lay quietly in the darkness beside Gustav's sleeping form. The urgency of his desire had been transferred to her in the most exciting way, and somewhere deep inside she knew that she had given as much as she had received until, spent and exhausted, they had lain silently in each other's arms while their heartbeats subsided gradually to resume their normal pace.

When Caroline awoke the Monday morning she found Gustav's side of the bed empty except for a folded sheet of crisp white paper on his pillow. She unfolded it carefully, but her heart was beating painfully in her throat when she read the words written in his firm, decisive handwriting.

'Caroline,' the note began abruptly without any preceding form of endearment, 'Last night, you must admit, was a revelation to us both, but don't forget that nothing lasts for ever. You're young, and I'm the first man to make love to you. If you are wise you won't place any significance on that and, I hope, you will remember that I shall no doubt be impatient to end our association once I have rid myself of the parasite my father once married.

'I shan't be home before six this evening, so delay dinner until seven. G. de L.'

A tear fell on to the paper, smudging the ink, then she crushed the note into a tight ball between her cold hands. Had she given away so much last night that he had felt it necessary to warn her off? she wondered as a wave of humiliation swept through her. At least he had possessed enough tact not to confront her personally with his suspicions, and for that she should be grateful, she supposed, but heaven only knew how she was going to cope with her futile emotions in future.

White-faced, she climbed out of bed and pulled on her robe to cover her nakedness where the bruises stood out on her white flesh as a painful reminder of the intimacy they had shared the night before. She ought to destroy his note, but she could not, and she unfolded it almost automatically before hiding it beneath some of her personal things in the dressing table drawer. If she ever considered stepping out of line during her stay at La Roche, then that note would act as a reminder not to bare her soul to a man who had made it clear that he had no interest in her other than a temporary physical attraction.

It was a long day for Caroline with plenty of time to consider her position, and to find the courage to face the man she had married two days ago. She had grown up, too, during those long hours of waiting for Gustav to return home from work, and she was proud of herself when she found that she could face him across the dinner table that evening with a cool, level glance that matched his own. Their conversation was brief and impersonal with nothing of real interest to say to each other, and a wide chasm developed between them which she felt incapable of bridging.

To her intense relief Gustav spent the evening in his study, and she was already asleep when he finally came to bed.

At the breakfast table the following morning the same uncomfortable silence threatened until Gustav pushed a cheque across the table towards her. She stared at it without comprehension for a moment, then she noticed that it was made out to her, and the amount written in figures made her eyes widen perceptibly.

'I want you to buy yourself a few suitable outfits to wear,' Gustav explained blandly as he helped himself to a second cup of coffee.

'I'm damned if I will!' she exploded before she could prevent herself.

'As my wife I demand that you shall be suitably clothed, and if you think I would waste a further cent on you if it were not for the sole purpose of appearing convincing to Isobel, then you're mistaken.'

His words lashed her with the stinging precision of a professionally wielded whip, and her body grew taut as she lowered her eyes before the fury in his gaze to say dully, 'You've made your point.'

'Thank heaven for that,' he remarked with biting sarcasm. 'I suggest you do your shopping today. It's quite likely that we shall have my undesirable family on our hands tomorrow.'

Caroline looked up sharply. 'You've heard from them?'

'Not directly, no, but I have my sources of information.' His eyes hardened as he glanced at her across the table. 'And for God's sake wipe that scared look off your face. It makes you look young and insecure, and that's all Isobel will need to make her suspect that our marriage is not what it's supposed to be.'

She swallowed convulsively and lowered her gaze. 'I'm sorry.'

'And whatever you do, don't cry,' he snapped cruelly when he glimpsed the suggestion of moisture in her eyes. 'If there's one thing I can't stand, then it's a woman who needs only the slightest provocation to bawl her eyes out.'

Several remarks sprang to mind, but she bit down hard on her quivering lip as she watched him swallow down his coffee and stalk out of the room. When the Jaguar sped down the drive moments later she picked up the cheque and stared at it with eyes that were angry enough to set fire to it. Her fingers tightened on the paper, but she fought down the temptation to tear it to shreds, and folded it instead before slipping it into the pocket of her tweed skirt.

Caroline had always dreamed of going on a shopping spree such as the one she went on that morning, but she felt certain that she would derive no pleasure from selecting an entire new wardrobe for the sole purpose of blinding Gustav's family to the truth, and she left the choice to a delighted saleslady who seemed to know exactly what was required, and what would suit her customer best.

Despite her initial displeasure, Caroline enjoyed the feel of the silk and fine wool garments against her skin. She had never owned anything this expensive, nor anything that seemed to suit her slender femininity to such perfection, and her enthusiasm increased when the saleslady suggested she should have her hair cut and styled to suit her new image.

A new image. Yes, she liked the idea. She was creating a new image to suit her status as Mrs Gustav de Leeuw. The *temporary* Mrs Gustav de Leeuw, she hastened to add to herself, and her mouth tightened with the stab of pain that shot through her.

Her Austin was loaded with parcels when she arrived at La Roche late that afternoon. Gustav had arrived home earlier that afternoon, but he was in his study and did not wish to be disturbed, Tilly told Caroline when she came out to help with the packages.

Alone in the bedroom she shared with Gustav, Caroline indulged in a leisurely bath before changing into one of her new outfits, and she selected a soft woollen dress with a wide collar which accentuated the smoothness of her slender throat. The colour was a pale blue that matched her eyes, and the lines were plain, yet elegant to suit her youthful figure. Her hair, cut shorter to hang just to her shoulders, was styled to lie in soft waves about her delicately contoured face, and the image she presented to herself in the mirror possessed a degree of calm sophistication which was quite startling. She no longer had that look of childish innocence about her; it had been replaced by the look of a woman who had experienced a man's passionate embraces, and a woman who was discovering the pain of loving unwisely.

'If there's one thing I can't stand then it's a woman who needs only the slightest provocation to bawl her eyes out,' Gustav's scathing remark returned to taunt her, and she hastily blinked back the stinging moisture in her eyes before going downstairs.

The sound of muffled voices coming from the direction of the living-room made her pause at the bottom of the stairs. The living-room door was closed to keep in the warmth of the fire which had been lit earlier that afternoon, and Caroline had no way of knowing whether Gustav's visitors had come to La Roche on business, or pleasure. Should she go in, or quietly disappear? It was difficult to know exactly what Gustav expected of her, but a woman's throaty laughter filled her with an intense curiosity, and she decided to take the chance that her arrival would not be considered untimely.

She crossed the hall and paused only for a moment to compose herself sufficiently before she opened the door and entered the living-room.

The conversation ceased abruptly, and the attention of the small group of people in the room was suddenly focussed on Caroline. There was surprise, at first, then a measure of curiosity, but when Gustav held out his hand towards her, two of his three companions seemed to be alerted to the significance of his gesture.

His smile was faintly sardonic as his fingers tightened

about Caroline's, and something in his eyes warned her not to protest when he drew her to his side and placed a possessive arm about her waist.

'Darling,' the endearment seemed to come naturally, and although it afforded her a spark of pleaure, she knew that it had been uttered for the benefit of those present. 'I would like you to meet Isobel, her son Russell, and Russell's wife Nicola.' Again there was that warning light in his eyes, then he transferred his gaze to the silent group observing them, and stated with a ring of triumph in his voice, 'Caroline is my wife.'

One could have heard a pin drop during the silence that followed Gustav's announcement, but the first one to recover herself was Isobel. Well preserved for her age, with only the slightest suggestion of grey in her raven-black hair, she rose to her feet in what could only be described as a queenly manner, then she raked Caroline from head to foot with dark, furious eyes before turning her attention back to Gustav.

'If this is some kind of joke, Gustav, then I suggest that you cease it at once,' Isobel ordered in her throaty, well-modulated voice. 'We all know of your aversity to marriage, and your preference to change your women friends as often almost as you change your suit.' Her disparaging glance raked Caroline once more before she demanded of Gustav, 'Who is this girl, and what's she doing here at La Roche, or have you now become indiscreet in your numerous affairs as well as imbecilic in selecting someone who's almost young enough to be your child?'

Isobel's disclosure angered Caroline and, her nervousness forgotten, she retorted, 'I'm not a child, and neither am I Gustav's mistress. I'm his wife, and I would thank you to remember that.'

Dark eyes burned into her and the scarlet mouth was drawn into a dangerously thin line. 'You're nothing but an impertinent hussy!'

'That will do, Isobel,' Gustav warned, his arm tightening almost protectively about Caroline's shaking form. 'Whether you like it or not, Caroline is my wife, and if you want written proof, then I'll give it to you.'

'You won't get away with this,' Isobel threatened in a furious whisper. 'I warn you, you won't get away with this!'

'Mother,' Russell intervened, rising from the sofa where he had lounged beside his young, pregnant wife, and crossing the room to his mother's side. 'This is a shock to us all, but let's not forget our manners in the process and neglect to offer Gustav and Caroline our congratulations.'

Surprisingly, Isobel took his advice, and after making a visible effort to control herself, she muttered something suitable. Caroline found it difficult to accept her congratulations as sincere, and she transferred her attention instead to Russell.

If one could have described him as a male replica of his mother, then that was how Caroline saw him. Tall, lean and dark, he possessed the same high-boned features, and she could not help noticing that he had received more than his fair share of good looks. There was something about him, however, that made her decide to tread warily in future in her dealings with Gustav's stepbrother.

CHAPTER SEVEN

CAROLINE never quite knew afterwards how she managed to survive through that long, tension-packed evening, but of Gustav's three relatives by marriage she preferred Nicola. Young, auburn-haired, and pretty, she appeared to have very little to say for herself, but it was obvious that she adored her suave, good-looking husband. It was also distressingly obvious that, like her husband, she had allowed herself to become totally dominated by her forceful mother-in-law, and as a result she had become rather a pathetic person whom Caroline could not help feeling sorry for.

When they were on their way to dinner that evening, Isobel halted abruptly in her stride as they crossed the dining hall, and demanded furiously, 'What's Lilian's portrait doing there?' She turned on Gustav, her eyes flashing fire. 'This was your idea, I suppose.'

'Actually it was mine,' Caroline intervened, drawing that fiery glance away from Gustav who stood motionless at her side.

'You will see to it that the servants remove it first thing in the morning,' Isobel instructed, but as she turned away Gustav's voice halted her.

'My mother's portrait will remain where it is,' he announced in cold, decisive tones. 'And whoever removes it will have to account to me for their actions.'

Caroline expected an explosion as their glances clashed but, miraculously, nothing happened, and they eventually sat down to a silent and somewhat strained meal.

'When were you married?' Isobel demanded of Gustav much later that evening, and although Caroline's insides contracted nervously, Gustav displayed no sign of discomfort.

'Believe it or not,' he said, passing Isobel her drink and seating himself on the arm of Caroline's chair, 'your arrival has interrupted our honeymoon. We were married only a few days ago. On Saturday, to be exact.'

Caroline's cheeks became flushed and her pulse quickened, but whether it was at the mention of the word 'honeymoon', or the sensual caress of those fingers that dipped with such daring beneath the collar of her dress, she could not say.

Moments later anger and embarrassment were valid enough reasons for staining her cheeks a deep red when Isobel remarked sarcastically, 'How inconvenient for you both!'

Gustav's caressing fingers stilled against Caroline's throat, and as she glanced up at him he said harshly, 'You blush charmingly, my dear, but the only remedy to counteract that is to ignore Isobel's remarks. She's the most tactless person I know.'

'Coming from someone as crude and uncouth as yourself, I take that as a compliment,' Isobel retaliated, her voice rising a pitch higher.

The situation was all at once explosive, and as Caroline's glance met Russell's, he said: 'Don't pay too much attention to all this, Caroline. Harmony in the home is something totally foreign when we're together as a ... er ... family.'

'Shut up, Russell!' Isobel snapped waspishly at her son. 'No one asked you to interfere.'

'Sorry, Mother,' he shrugged in a subdued manner.

'What are you, Russell?' Gustav demanded harshly. 'A man or a mouse?'

'He knows which side his bread is buttered, and that's more than I can say for you!' Isobel retorted in a voice that only barely concealed her fury.

'That's what's annoyed you all along, isn't it?' Gustav remarked contemptuously. 'I've never yet had to turn to you for anything, and I'm damned if I ever will.'

Dark eyes flashed now with undisguised fury. 'You're a pompous bastard, and I should have had you thrown out of this house on the day I married your father!'

Caroline raised her anxious glance to Gustav's, but his rugged features remained expressionless as he held the glance of the woman seated close to him.

'Too bad my father had a little more sense than you credited him with,' his icy voice sliced through the silence, and it was at this point that Caroline attempted to intervene.

'Perhaps I should make a pot of coffee,' she suggested, rising to her feet and casting a wary glance about the room.

'That's an excellent idea, Caroline,' Gustav remarked caustically when her glance met his. 'And make it strong. Isobel needs to be fortified after all the energy she's burned up this evening.'

'Would you like to come with me, Nicola?' Caroline questioned the other girl hastily before Isobel could retaliate with yet another stinging remark.

'Yes, I——'

'You stay where you are, Nicola,' Isobel's angry voice interrupted Nicola, who was in the process of levering herself up out of the sofa. 'You know what the doctor said about taking things easy, and not standing about too much.'

Feeling sorry for Nicola, Caroline glanced at Isobel and said irritably, 'We do have chairs in the kitchen, if I'm not mistaken.'

'Yes,' the older woman snapped. 'Hard and uncomfortable chairs which are totally unsuitable for someone in Nicola's delicate condition.'

Caroline's eyes met Nicola's, and an apologetic little smile hovered on the girl's quivering mouth. 'I'm sorry.'

Deciding that it was best not to be too persistent, Caroline cast her a final sympathetic glance before taking herself off to the kitchen.

Her nerves unravelled themselves to a certain extent while she was in the kitchen, but when she returned to the living-room with the tray of coffee the argument was still in full swing. Insults and accusations were hurled back and forth across the room with the rapidity of machine-gun fire, and it ceased only for a few brief moments while they drank their coffee before it was resumed once more.

It was Gustav who finally brought the unpleasant scene to an end by saying, 'We're beginning to repeat ourselves, Isobel. I suggest we retire for the night and, if necessary, resume this discussion tomorrow evening.'

'You've a hide as thick as a rhinoceros,' she flung yet another accusation at him.

'Your insults are beginning to bore me, Isobel, most especially when they should be directed at yourself,' he replied cuttingly before he cast a disparaging glance at Russell, who had not dared to intervene since his mother had shut him up so rudely. 'Be a man this once,' Gustav ordered, 'and remove your mother from my sight.'

'You forget that this is my home,' Isobel stated regally.

'It's mine as well,' Gustav reminded her with glacial coldness. 'For as long as I care to remain, La Roche is my home.'

'Come on, Mother,' Russell found the courage to speak. 'This argument is leading nowhere, and we're all tired.'

'For once you're right,' Isobel acknowledged. 'I *am* tired, and Nicola must be exhausted.' She transferred her attention to her daughter-in-law and rose to her feet. 'Come along, child, it's time you were in bed.'

The trio departed without another word, and as the door closed behind them Gustav turned towards the stinkwood dresser in the corner.

'I could do with a drink.'

'So could I,' Caroline admitted readily. 'Something strong and lethal.'

'At your age wine is considered lethal enough,' he smiled faintly, handing her a glass of vintage wine and swallowing down what appeared to be a neat whisky.

'Don't you bring my age into it as well!' she retorted angrily.

'Isobel was right, though,' he observed, regarding her with narrowed unfathomable eyes. 'I *am* almost old enough to be your father.'

'Don't be silly!'

'Would you have liked me for a father?'

'Certainly not!'

'You prefer me to be your lover?'

Her pulse quickened, and she found that she could no longer sustain his glance. 'I would prefer you to change the subject.'

'Very well,' he shrugged, placing his empty glass on

the mantelshelf and thrusting his hands into his pockets. He surveyed her intently for a moment, then his eyes travelled over her with a sensual intimacy that quickened the flow of blood through her veins, and tainted her cheeks a rosy pink. 'I like your new hairstyle, and I like that dress. It makes you look soft and feminine, and utterly desirable.'

'Please, Gustav,' she begged, turning away to hide what he might see in her yes, and sipping at her wine in an effort to steady herself.

'You really do blush very easily.'

Caroline ignored his remark, and changed the subject. 'Is this evening an example of how we're going to spend every evening for the next month and a half?'

'It's anybody's guess how we'll end up spending our evenings, but when Isobel and I get together there's bound to be some sort of eruption.'

'Has it always been that way?' she asked tentatively, turning to face him now that she had her feelings under control once more.

'Always,' he confirmed abruptly.

'I do feel sorry for Nicola,' she murmured, seating herself on the arm of a chair and staring down at the crimson liquid in her glass. 'She's totally repressed and dominated.'

'She had no business getting herself into that position.'

The callousness of his remark made her flinch inwardly. 'We can't all be strong, Gustav.'

'Except for a few blushes I didn't notice you quaking under Isobel's influence.'

'That's probably because I'm not her daughter-in-law, and you're not Russell.'

'Thank God for that!'

She looked up then and asked a little warily, 'What happens next?'

'You come to bed with me.'

'I wasn't referring to that, and you know it,' she retorted angrily, lowering her eyes before the glittering mockery in his glance.

'It's a much more interesting subject, don't you think?'

'Be serious, please,' she begged without looking up. 'What does happen next?'

'We wait.'

'Wait?' She raised questioning eyes once more to meet the onslaught of his disturbing glance. 'What do we wait for?'

'For them to make the first move.'

'It sounds like a deadly game of chess,' Caroline spoke her thoughts out aloud.

'And don't underestimate your opponent,' he warned, approaching her chair with a purposeful look in his gleaming eyes that made her put down her glass and jump to her feet to move beyond his reach.

'I think I *will* go up to bed,' she announced hastily, but she could have bitten off her tongue the next minute when she saw the mockery deepen in his eyes.

'A delightful suggestion,' he agreed, and she wished suddenly that the ancient floorboards of La Roche would cave in beneath her, but they remained solid beneath her feet.

They went upstairs in silence with Gustav putting off the lights as they went, but once they reached the privacy of their bedroom his mood seemed to have altered and he appeared to be engrossed in his thoughts.

Caroline was brushing her hair before going to bed when he emerged from the dressing-room in a short towelling robe that exposed his long, muscular limbs. He had nothing on beneath it, she was almost certain of that, and every nerve in her body reacted to his nearness when he came up behind her and met her wary glance in the dressing-table mirror.

His question startled her at first, but when she began to suspect that he doubted her capabilities, she became defensive and angry.

'I shall have to, shan't I?'

'What's that supposed to mean?' he demanded, his dark brows drawing together in a frown.

She did not answer him at once, but put down her brush and rose to her feet, moving away from him as she did so to lessen the advantage he had over her in height.

'If I were a horse,' she said at last in a tight little voice, 'then I would say you've backed an awful lot of money on me, and that places you in a position to demand satisfaction, doesn't it?'

'That's right,' he acknowledged harshly, his hands hurting her shoulders when he came up behind her and turned her roughly to face him, and the glittering fury in his eyes would have frightened her if she was not so intent upon hiding the feelings his nearness aroused as he added gratingly, 'I bought you lock, stock and barrel, and I always demand my money's worth.'

'I shall feel sorry for you one day when you discover that money can't buy you the thing you'll want most.'

'Such as?' he demanded cynically.

'Love.'

'Love is an overrated emotion I have no time for,' he answered with a sneer. 'All I shall ever need is a woman in my bed from time to time, and women like that can always be bought.'

'You're disgusting!' she cried, trying to free herself, but his hands merely tightened mercilessly on her shoulders, bruising the soft flesh.

'I bought you, didn't I?'

Caroline flinched as if he had struck her, and her eyes became black pools of pain in her white face. 'You know very well that I'm not that kind of woman.'

'I had to pin a marriage certificate to my cheque, yes, but it amounts to the same thing,' he replied with biting sarcasm, 'and like most women you were willing to be bought.'

She drew a shuddering breath and resorted to anger once again as her only defence. 'Don't make me despise you any more than I already do.'

'You may despise me all you like,' he laughed harshly, dragging her against him and holding her prisoner against the hard wall of his chest. 'You're really quite beautiful when you're angry, and it merely makes me want you more.'

She turned her face away as he lowered his head, but his hand fastened on to her hair, and her cry of protest was stifled beneath the hard, suffocating onslaught of his mouth. She tried to fight against the steel-like strength of his arms, but already the blood was pounding through her veins, and her treacherous body arched towards his in a way she knew she would despise herself for later. His touch was possessive on the soft curves of her slender figure, and she was only vaguely conscious of being stripped of her silk robe and flimsy nightdress, then the edge of the bed was behind her knees, and she went down with Gustav on top of her.

His hands on her responsive flesh excited her beyond reason, but when his mouth followed the destructive path of his hands, a moan of pure ecstasy escaped her.

The words 'I love you' hovered precariously on her burning, swollen lips, but they were fortunately never uttered when they were interrupted by the sound of their bedroom door being opened. Gustav muttered something that sounded quite frightening, then he raised his head, and turned towards whoever it was who had shown such a total disregard for their privacy. Whether by accident or design, Caroline never quite knew which, his body shielded hers from the prying eyes of the intruder, but over his broad shoulder her startled glance encountered a still fully clothed Isobel.

'I'm sorry,' she smiled, but there was cold hatred in those dark eyes. 'I had no idea that this room was occupied.'

Gustav's shoulders moved angrily beneath his towelling robe, and his voice was chilling when he spoke. 'Next time I suggest you knock and wait until you're asked to come in.'

Isobel's smile became a sneer but, surprisingly, she left as abruptly as she had entered.

For a moment neither Gustav nor Caroline moved, then he sat up and glanced down at her mockingly, making her more concerned now about her nakedness than the embarrassment of having Isobel walk in on them.

'She was lying!' she snapped angrily, diverting his attention away from her as she dragged the bedcover about her and pushed herself up on to one elbow. 'She couldn't have missed seeing the light under the door.'

'That little incident was planned to ascertain whether we share the same room, and whether our knot of wedded bliss is tied securely.'

His tone was matter-of-fact, giving Caroline the distinct impression that the entire incident had been planned, and her eyes sparkled with instant fury at the thought that he had callously manipulated her into this humiliating incident she had just lived through.

'I think you're the most revolting people I've ever met, and if you touch me now I think I'll scream!' she announced when at last she found her voice.

'That won't be necessary,' Gustav smiled caustically, getting to his feet. 'You have a delectable body, but my interest has lasted only long enough to convince Isobel that we're as married as I want her to believe we are.'

The blood surged into her face, then it drained away to leave her deathly pale as she demanded hoarsely, 'What kind of man are you?'

'I know what I want, and I'll stop at nothing to get it. Here . . .' he added, picking up her nightdress and flinging it on to the bed beside her. 'Put this on and get into bed. You've served your purpose for tonight.'

If he had struck her physically then she could not have been more stunned and, lowering her lashes to hide the stark pain in her eyes, she snatched up the flimsy garment beside her and, slipping it over her head, fled into the dressing-room before she destroyed the little that remained of her dignity by bursting into tears.

She would never give him the opportunity again to humiliate her in this manner, she decided some time later when she lay beside him staring into the darkness. *Never!* She had learnt a valuable lesson that evening, and she was not likely to forget it in a hurry.

When Caroline awoke the following morning Gustav had already left for the office. A half hour later, dressed in warm slacks and a sweater with comfortable walking shoes on her feet, she slipped her arms into the sleeves of her raincoat and went downstairs, but in the hall she ran into Nicola.

'I'm sorry about last night,' the girl apologised shyly,

and for one startled moment Caroline thought that she was referring to Isobel's untimely visit to their bedroom, then Nicola set her mind at rest with, 'I'm not really as delicate as Isobel would like people to believe, but it's easier to follow the line of least resistance.'

'Why, Nicola?' Caroline questioned softly. 'You have the right to make your own decisions.'

'You don't understand,' Nicola sighed, her hazel eyes filling with moisture. 'I love Russell, despite the way he dances attendance to his mother, and I don't want to lose him.'

Caroline's glance sharpened. 'Why on earth should you lose him?'

'Surely you've formed some idea since last night of the influence his mother has over him?'

Caroline stared a little blankly at the girl, who could not be more than a year or two older than herself, then her eyes began to widen with growing understanding. 'Are you suggesting that, if she decided to send you packing, he would let you go?'

'Without a murmur,' Nicola confessed bitterly, then her anxious glance travelled upwards towards the sound of light footsteps coming down the stairs. 'That's Isobel,' she added in a frightened whisper. 'I'm not supposed to be talking to you. She calls it fraternising with the enemy.'

'Nicola?' Isobel questioned sharply moments later when she rounded the bend in the stairs. She paused briefly, her cold glance taking in Caroline's presence, then she hurried down into the hall and focussed her attention once more on Nicola. 'What are you doing down here so early in the morning?' she demanded suspiciously.

'I came down for a glass of milk, and I was asking

Caroline the way to the kitchen.'

'The kitchen is that way,' Isobel told her abruptly, pointing across the hall towards the passage leading off it.

'So Caroline was telling me,' Nicola lied and, casting an imploring glance in Caroline's direction, she murmured, 'Excuse me,' and hurried away.

Caroline smothered the sick feeling in her breast and turned away, but a slender hand caught hold of her arm to detain her.

'I want to speak to you,' said Isobel and, removing her hand from Caroline's arm, she gestured towards the living-room. Caroline felt like telling her to go to the devil, but changed her mind and entered the room ahead of Isobel. 'Why did you marry my stepson?' Isobel demanded of Caroline the moment she had closed the door behind them.

The directness of Isobel's question startled Caroline momentarily, but she recovered swiftly to say, 'I married him for the usual reasons people marry each other.'

'It wouldn't be for love,' Isobel sneered. 'Gustav hasn't one loving hair on his head, so it has to be for some other reason.' A cynical smile curved her scarlet mouth as her cold glance travelled over Caroline. 'I'm told he's a superb lover.'

'You surely don't expect me to reply to that, Isobel?' Caroline demanded, choking back her anger.

'My, but how discreet we are this morning!' Isobel mocked her, but Caroline was determined to control her temper, even though she could do nothing about the wave of colour that swept her cheeks.

'I'm always discreet, Isobel, and I would certainly never intrude on anyone's privacy without an invitation.'

'If you knew Gustav as well as I do, then you wouldn't trust him an inch.' Those dark eyes narrowed speculatively. 'Did he pay you a handsome amount to marry him?'

'He paid me the compliment of asking me to be his wife, and that was all,' Caroline retorted stiffly, glad that at least this was true, then she changed the subject. 'Will you have breakfast now, or would you like to wait until Russell comes down?'

Isobel gestured impatiently with her hands. 'Russell seldom rises early, so I'll take breakfast now.'

'I'll send one of the servants to attend to you in the breakfast room,' said Caroline, brushing past Isobel and heading towards the door.

'I'll summon someone myself,' Isobel replied haughtily. 'This is my home, after all, and don't you forget that.'

Caroline's fingers tightened on the polished brass door-handle and a look of determination flashed in her eyes as she turned to face the older woman. 'As I'm Gustav's wife this is my home too, but if you take a secret delight in tugging bell ropes, then please yourself. I'm going for a walk.'

She had flung open the door and was crossing the hall when she heard Isobel choking on the words 'Impertinent hussy', but she did not care and, opening the heavy oak door, she stepped outside.

It was a cold, cloudy day with the rain coming down in a fine, soft spray, but Caroline barely noticed as she walked briskly down the drive and out through the wrought iron gates. She was some distance down the tree-lined avenue before she paused to wonder where she was going, but she shrugged her shoulders in a somewhat fatalistic manner and walked on once more.

The rain on her face seemed to cleanse her soul of bitterness and anger, but nothing, it seemed, could rid her of the leaden feeling in her breast. Her mind, unleashed, leapt from one incident to the next, rejecting, dissecting, and finally accepting her fate with the realisation that, no matter how much Gustav might yet hurt her, she would always love him.

A car drew up alongside her, but she was too deep in thought to pay much attention until the door on the passenger side was opened and a man's voice called her name. She turned and stared, then a smile lit up her face as she accepted the unspoken invitation to get into the car.

'It's good to see you, Dennis,' she said sincerely as he drove a little farther before parking his car along the side of the road where it broadened for the purpose of those who wished to admire the view down into the valley.

'I'm on my way back from visiting one of the bank's clients, and I couldn't believe my eyes when I saw you walking along in the rain,' he explained, turning in his seat to face her. For a long moment he was silent, then he said: 'I never thought I'd see you again.'

Sadness lurked in her eyes as she met the steady regard of the man she had, not so long ago, hoped to marry. Seeing him now afforded her no special pleasure, no glowing warmth—only a vague delight at meeting someone who now meant no more than a friend to her.

'We had said goodbye to a life together, but that doesn't mean we can't be friends,' she offered tentatively, but he brushed her words aside with an angry gesture.

'We can never be friends, Caroline. Not now that I know what a fool I was to have let you go.'

'Our marriage would never have worked, Dennis,' she said, averting her gaze. 'I never really loved you, and I know that now.'

'It was a shock to me when I heard that you'd married Gustav de Leeuw,' he told her in that same angry tone. 'He's so much older than you.'

'What do eighteen years matter when you love someone?'

'It will matter when he's senile and you're still young enough to want to enjoy life.'

'I won't have you talking like that, do you hear me!' she cried angrily, her eyes blazing in a way he had never noticed before, and Dennis seemed to realise that he had overstepped the mark.

'I'm sorry, Caroline,' he murmured apologetically. 'Jealousy has made me spiteful, so don't blame me too much.'

'I think I'd better go.'

'Wait!' he stopped her as her hand reached for the catch on the door. 'When will I see you again?'

'There's no purpose in our meeting again,' she told him quietly, looking up into those dark eyes which had once had the power to make her melt inwardly, and feeling nothing except a slight irritation. 'You said yourself that we could never be friends, and if we can't meet as friends, then it's best that we don't see each other again.'

He drew away from her, and nodded. 'You're right, of course.'

'It's the best way, believe me, and I——'

A car drove past, and Caroline's nerves tightened when she recognised Russell's dark profile in the driver's seat. Had he seen her, she wondered, or had he been too busy negotiating the bend in the road to notice?

'What is it?' Dennis asked, taking in her troubled expression, and she pulled herself together swiftly.

'That was my husband's stepbrother who just drove past.'

'So what?' Dennis wanted to know.

'So nothing!' she snapped irritably. 'I just happened to notice him, that's all, and it's reminded me that I must get back to La Roche.'

'Caroline . . .'

'It was nice seeing you again, Dennis, but this time it's really goodbye,' she interrupted adamantly and, getting out of his car, she walked back the way she had come, and did not look back when she heard him start his car and drive away.

If she had doubted her feelings before, then she was certain now. She had never loved Dennis, and the incident which had led up to their separation could not have occurred at a more convenient moment in time, for it had saved her from making the biggest mistake of her life.

'Was marrying Gustav not a far bigger mistake?' her sober mind questioned, but the question remained unanswered as a car drove up beside her some minutes later for the second time that morning.

'Hello there!' Russell greeted her, leaning across to wind down the window on the passenger side. 'Want a lift home?'

Her hair clung damply to her forehead, but she shook her head. 'Thank you, but I would prefer to walk.'

'Suit yourself, honey,' he shrugged, a sly look entering his eyes. 'But it isn't exactly the right weather for walking, is it?'

What did he mean by that? she wondered as she said: 'I've always enjoyed walking in the rain.'

'See you later, then,' he said, flashing her the most peculiar smile as he wound up the window.

Moments later, as she stood watching him drive back towards La Roche, she knew for certain that he had seen her in the car with Dennis. The question was, however, what was he going to do about it and, worse still, how would Gustav react to the news if it should be passed on to him.

'Damn!' she muttered, kicking at a pebble in her frustration. She felt quite certain that Isobel had sent him after her to spy on her. No other errand would have brought him back so quickly to La Roche, and no one else would have thought up anything so lousy.

She would have to be far more careful in future if she did not want to jeopardise Gustav's plans, Caroline realised dismally. Isobel and her son were going all out to get what they wanted, and she had just had a demonstration of how little they cared what methods they employed in their efforts to reach their goal.

CHAPTER EIGHT

IT was during lunch that same day that Caroline found Russell's speculative glance resting on her from time to time, and he smiled once, giving the distinct impression that he shared a secret with her. 'He knows,' she thought, and not for a moment afterwards did she doubt that he had seen her in the car with Dennis. What he intended to do with that information still remained a mystery to her, but he had the look of a man with an ace up his sleeve which he had every intention of using to its best advantage.

When Isobel went upstairs to rest, insisting that Nicola did the same, Caroline found herself alone at the lunch table with Russell, and it was curiosity alone that made her remain there to indulge in a second cup of tea.

Russell lit a cigarette, the first one she had seen him smoke, and leaned back in his chair to observe her quite openly now that they were alone.

'You know, you're not at all the sort of girl I imagined would succeed in making Gustav change his mind about remaining a bachelor.'

This was not at all what she had expected and, startled, she said with some sarcasm, 'Really?'

'I meant no offence, I assure you,' he hastened to add. 'It's just that old Gustav always seemed to prefer tall, sexy-looking women, and although you're attractive, you're so very different from them.'

A warning bell clanged in her mind. 'Take care,' it

seemed to say and, doing just that, she said: 'I suppose a man looks for something different when it comes to choosing a wife.'

Russell was silent for a moment, then a sly smile curved his weak mouth. 'Did you know that Gustav had to find himself a wife before the fifteenth of next month?'

'If you're referring to the stipulation in your step-father's will, then the answer is yes, I do know about it.'

His smile vanished. 'He told you?'

'We have no secrets from each other,' she replied sweetly, taking a sip of her tea and observing him over the rim of her cup with a hint of humour in her eyes.

'Doesn't it bother you to think that he might have married you for that reason alone?' he questioned, his narrowed eyes intent upon her as he exhaled a cloud of smoke towards the ceiling, but her own glance did not waver for one second.

'If you're trying to sow doubt in my mind, then you're not succeeding, Russell.'

'I'd think about it if I were you,' he persisted, his glance shifting insolently towards the soft curve of her breasts beneath her sweater. 'You're an attractive wench, but you're not his type at all, and knowing old Gustav the way I do, I wouldn't put it past him to marry someone merely to keep the infernal family business to himself.'

'He has more right to it than you have,' Caroline remarked swiftly, instantly on the defensive for the man she loved.

'Ah, but you see, old Regardt didn't consider him a suitable candidate,' Russell argued with a cold smile, very like his mother's, hovering about his lips.

'Regardt, I presume, is Gustav's late father?'

'That's right,' he nodded, observing her intently once more, and she realised her mistake moments before he continued to speak. 'For someone who's supposed to be Gustav's wife you know very little about the family, it seems.'

'I know enough,' she tried to cover up her error, 'but you seem to forget that we've only been married a few days.'

'But you knew him before your marriage, surely?'

'Yes, of course.'

'How long?' he rapped out suspiciously.

'Long enough,' she prevaricated, wishing that she could slap that silly smile off his face.

'It was a whirlwind courtship, was it?'

'Not exactly,' she replied coldly, rising to her feet in a determined effort to end this conversation which had told her nothing of what she had hoped to find out. 'If you'll excuse me, then I think I'll go upstairs as well.'

Russell rose to his feet, and for one terrifying moment she thought he was going to follow her to pursue the subject, but he remained where he was, his eyes following her from the room as she hurried into the hall and up the stairs to her room.

Caroline looked upon Gustav's return to La Roche that evening with a feeling of dread. If Russell was out to make mischief, then he would do so when Gustav was home, and what better time than when they all came together in the living-room for a drink before Gustav went upstairs to shower and change for dinner. She cringed inwardly at the thought of what might occur, but she was like someone caught in a trap from which there was no escape, and as the hours passed with terrifying swiftness, her insides knotted themselves into a tight ball which became lodged at the pit of her stomach.

When Gustav finally arrived home that evening, Caroline was numb with nerves, but what she had dreaded did not occur, and her tension had increased almost to breaking point when it was time to sit down to dinner. She barely touched her food, and the little she did try to swallow down seemed to lodge somewhere between her throat and her stomach.

It was between the second and the third course that Russell caught her eye, and she knew, irrevocably, that this was the moment she had dreaded all evening.

'By the way, Caroline,' Russell began with a casualness which could not be faulted, 'was that you I saw down the road this morning, sitting in a car with some fellow?'

All eyes were suddenly focussed on Caroline, but it was Gustav's hard, expressionless face that swam before her eyes.

'Yes, it was,' she confessed without taking her eyes from Gustav's. 'I was out walking when Dennis drove past. He stopped, and we talked for a while,' she explained, but her explanation was directed at Gustav, and not Russell.

'I hope you invited him over one evening.'

Caroline stared at Gustav a little blankly for a moment, then understanding dawned, and she entered into the scene he was enacting for the benefit of the others present.

'I did, yes, and he said he'd give us a ring when he had a free evening,' she lied with a glibness that amazed even herself.

'Who is this Dennis you're speaking of?' Isobel demanded from the other end of the table, her eyes, like a hawk's, watching them intently.

'He's a mutual friend who had quite a hand in bringing Caroline and myself together,' Gustav explained before pinning Caroline down once more with his direct gaze. 'Isn't that so, darling?'

Caroline felt a little sick inside, but she could not help thinking that there was some truth in his statement. If Dennis had not behaved so stuffily, she would not have been free to marry Gustav and, smiling faintly, she said: 'That is so, yes.'

'Does this Dennis character make a habit of picking you up for a chummy little chat in his car?' Russell wanted to know, and the sarcasm in his voice made her hackles rise.

'Certainly not!' Caroline exclaimed hotly.

'Don't pay any attention to him, my dear,' Gustav intervened smoothly. 'He'll change his mind about Dennis once he's met him.'

Caroline glanced at Gustav, and his tawny eyes issued a clear warning not to pursue the subject. They were treading on dangerous ground, and it was best to step off it as quickly as possible.

The topic of conversation was changed, but this time it was Caroline who observed Russell unobtrusively. His face bore the look of a man who had lost, but when she looked up to find Gustav's cold eyes resting on her, she knew that Russell had not failed after all.

Despite the few sarcastic remarks which were passed, it turned out to be a quieter evening than the one before, but the storm broke over Caroline's head later that evening when she emerged from the bathroom to find Gustav, his jacket and tie discarded, pacing the floor of their bedroom like a restless, angry animal.

He reached her side in a few lithe strides to take her shoulders in a bone-crushing grip, and fear churned through her at the thunderous look on his face.

'What the devil did you think you were doing, meeting Dennis what's-his-name behind my back?' he demanded harshly.

'His name is Dennis Lindsay,' she replied, attempting to remain calm, 'and I told you we met quite by chance.'

'That's a likely story,' he snarled derisively.

'It's nevertheless the truth.'

His hands tightened on her shoulders and she bit down hard on her lip in an effort not to cry out as he demanded furiously, 'Do you realise how easily you could have ruined my plans with your foolish behaviour?'

'It wasn't a planned meeting, Gustav,' she explained once again, wincing inwardly at the numb pain shooting into her arms. 'We met by accident, and I didn't think there was any harm in stopping for a moment to chat to him.'

A cynical smile curved his hard mouth. 'Did you enjoy reviving the sweet memories of your past?'

'What do you mean?' she asked stupidly, unable to look away from the blazing fury in his eyes.

'Oh, come now, Caroline,' he laughed cynically. 'Do you expect me to believe that you did nothing more than hold hands and talk?'

The blood surged into her cheeks, then drained away to leave her a deathly white, and she no longer made an effort to hide her anger as she flung her head back defiantly and hissed up at him, 'You have a filthy mind, Gustav!'

His mouth swooped down on to hers with a precision that drew a startled response from her, and he did not let up until he felt her quivering lips part beneath his.

'Did his kisses arouse you as mine do?' he demanded at last, his warm mouth exploring the slender smoothness of her throat with devastating effects while his hands moulded her to him with a sensuality that shattered the barriers of resistance she had tried so desperately to erect. 'Did his touch make you tremble with desire?' he continued to taunt her.

'Gustav, I swear to you——'

'Swear?' He raised his head, and the look of contempt in his eyes made her cringe inwardly. 'From the time the world began women have sworn loyalty to their husbands on various sacred objects, but they conveniently forget about it the moment someone else crosses their horizon.'

'No, that's not true!' she protested anxiously, desperate now to make him see the truth, but his hard, glittering eyes burned down into hers with renewed contempt, and the hand he had raised to her throat tightened until she knew a genuine fear that he was about to squeeze the life-giving breath from her body.

'I never asked you to swear loyalty to me,' he stated arrogantly. 'I bought your loyalty, and that's where the difference comes in. You owe it to me, and I demand it of you.'

Her anger was stronger than her fear at that moment and, forcing the words past the pressure exerted on her throat, she said huskily, 'You don't have to remind me that you bought my loyalty, and you have it for what it's worth. I'll help you get what you want even if it kills me, and after that I never want to see you again for as long as I live!'

The pressure on her throat relaxed, but a cynical smile played about his mouth. 'That suits me perfectly, but until then, my dear Caroline, I shall require the pleasure of your company in my bed.'

'You fiend! I hate you!' she spat out the words, but he lifted her with ease despite her flailing arms and legs, and carried her towards the bed.

'Go ahead, you little spitfire,' he laughed harshly, dropping her on to the soft folds of the bed and following her down to pin her beneath the weight of his body. 'Go ahead and hate me all you please.'

His derisive laughter rang tauntingly in her ears as he observed her futile efforts to escape him and, like an insect wriggling on a pin, he held her there until she had exhausted herself. Only then did his lips claim hers, and he plundered their softness with a practised sensuality which she tried desperately to resist until his hands slipped inside her silk robe to explore her supple, responsive flesh.

'Leave me alone! Please, leave me alone!' she groaned, clinging to the remnants of her fast fading control.

'I can't do that,' he murmured, burying his face in the scented hollow between her softly rounded breasts. 'Not when you want me as much as I want you.'

A denial sprang to her lips, but it remained unuttered as his caresses inflamed her with a desire only he could arouse in her. She tried to fight against it, but what was the use when every nerve and sinew in her body wanted his caresses to continue. She despised herself for her weakness, and for showing so clearly her need of him, but even as this thought flashed through her mind, her fingers fumbled with the tiny pearl buttons down the front of his expensive silk shirt until her hands encountered the muscled flesh of his hair-roughened chest. His own hand went down to the buckle of his belt, and seconds later their bodies melted together in a passionate embrace that drove every vestige of thought from her mind. Drugged with desire, her mouth sought his, then nothing mattered beyond the intense pleasure which his thrusting body aroused.

During the days that followed Caroline was subjected to Gustav's taunting reminders of that night when she had shown so clearly her need of him. She came to dread the nights when he would subdue her with his love-making, and she hated the days as the tension increased at La Roche to a point where she felt like screaming.

She could not talk to Isobel, for the woman tried in every conceivable way to twist her words and create an atmosphere of unpleasantness. Contrary to Isobel's behaviour, Russell's manner seemed to encourage a familiarity which Caroline tried to avoid at all costs, but somehow he was always there, touching her and flattering her, and always when Gustav was within sight. It was done very subtly and cleverly, but Caroline began to suspect that it was all planned to create a doubtful impression. What he hoped to achieve remained a mystery to her, but she had no doubt that she would find out in time.

Nicola was the only one Caroline could talk to without the fear of having her words misinterpreted or twisted to someone else's advantage, but the poor girl was seldom out from under Isobel's watchful eyes.

Caroline found Nicola walking in the garden one morning towards the end of their third week at La Roche, and her eyes automatically searched beyond Nicola.

'I'm alone,' Nicola assured her with a shy smile. 'Isobel slept badly last night, and she's staying in bed a while longer this morning.'

'Thank heaven for that!' Caroline could not help sighing.

'I don't blame you for not liking her,' Nicola remarked when she saw that look of guilt flash across Caroline's sensitive features. 'I'm not particularly fond of her myself.'

'She reminds me of a vulture biding its time before it swoops down to claim what is left of the kill,' Caroline muttered with a grimace.

'How very apt,' Nicola laughed, but she sobered almost at once. 'That's just what she's doing, of course. Biding her time before she swoops down to claim what she feels is hers.' Her serious glance met Caroline's. 'She means to have La Roche as well as Protea Marine Engineering, you know.'

An uncontrollable little shiver coursed its way up Caroline's spine, but her chin rose involuntarily in a gesture of defiance. 'There's no way she can get the business now that Gustav is married, and La Roche will always be his home.'

'Don't underestimate her, Caroline,' Nicola warned as they seated themselves on the bench beneath the shade of the old oak tree. 'She's very clever, and when she's desperate, she's deadly.'

'Desperate?' Caroline was instantly on the alert. 'In what way is she desperate?'

Nicola shook her dark head and looked away guiltily. 'Forgive me. I've said too much already, but I must remind you that the will states clearly that Gustav must be married and living with his wife to claim his inheritance.'

Caroline's glance sharpened, but she did not pursue the subject. She would have thought much less of Nicola had she not shown some form of loyalty towards her husband and his mother, but it certainly made her wonder just what still lay in store for Gustav and herself. She had never paid much attention to the latter half of that stipulation in the will, but she would have to give it a great deal more thought in future, for something warned her that this was what Isobel and her son were aiming at—a separation between Gustav and herself.

'Would you like to make your home here, Nicola?' Caroline asked eventually when the silence lengthened uncomfortably.

'If I had a choice I would return to Namibia today,' Nicola admitted sadly. 'I was born there, it's where Russell and I met, and I would like my baby to be born there.'

'Have you discussed this with Russell?'

'Many times, but he wants what his mother wants, and nothing else matters to him,' Nicola sighed, clasping her hands in her lap. 'They've talked of nothing else these past months but of Gustav's dethronement, as they call it, and I almost laughed out loud at the look on their faces when we arrived here and Gustav introduced you as his wife.'

'You'd think, they would give up and be satisfied with what they have,' Caroline observed dryly.

'Not Isobel and Russell,' Nicola shook her head adamantly. 'They'll always want more, and they won't rest until they get what they want.'

It was a disturbing end to their conversation, but Caroline had no idea how soon she would become involved in their plot to displace Gustav.

When they all came together for tea out on the terrace that morning, Caroline foolishly mentioned that she had some shopping to do.

'Why don't you drive Caroline in to town this morning, Russell?' Isobel suggested sweetly, and Caroline knew at once that Russell's manner of late had been prompted by his mother as part of their strategy.

'Oh, no, that won't be necessary,' she protested. 'I have my own——'

'I'd be delighted to give you a lift,' Russell interrupted smoothly, his warm glance playing over her with that

familiarity she found so despicable. 'I have a little business to attend to, and it would be silly going in two
cars,' he added convincingly.

Nicola nodded her approval, totally oblivious of anything untoward in the situation, and, not wanting to
awaken her suspicions, Caroline accepted Russell's offer
of a lift, but she would gladly have flung it back in his
face.

It was the most annoying trip into town which Caroline had ever experienced. She continually had to dis-
engage her hand from his, or remove his hand from her
knee, and she had never felt more relieved than when
they had parted company in the busy city centre after
arranging where they would meet an hour later.

Caroline took her time purchasing the few personal
items she required, delaying as much as possible her
return to where Russell had said he would be waiting
for her, but there was no way she could avoid the journey back to La Roche with that despicable man for
company.

With her parcels on the back seat of Russell's
Mercedes, she sat stiffly and silently beside him, but
when he parked the car on a quiet stretch of road near
Constantia, she turned to face him and asked sharply,
'Why are you stopping?'

'I like the view of the mountain from here.'

His smile was broad, but it was not the mountain he
was observing with such a calculating warmth in his
eyes, it was herself, and her skin began to crawl with
distaste.

'I think we should get back to La Roche,' she said
coldly. 'It's close on lunch time.'

'There's no hurry,' he argued, sliding his arm along
the back of the seat and leaning towards her with that

familiarity she disliked so intensely. 'I'm beginning to see why Gustav married you. You're really quite beautiful.'

His fingers caressed her cheek, and she jerked her head away. 'Please, don't do that.'

'Your skin is so soft,' he murmured, and before she could guess his intentions, his arms were about her.

'Let me go at once, Russell!' she ordered, freezing in his clasp.

'Don't be so standoffish, honey,' he laughed, and then she was fighting like the very devil to evade his lips and hands.

'Behave yourself, Russell!' she exclaimed furiously when at last she managed to thrust him from her. 'If you don't behave yourself I'll get out and walk the rest of the way!'

'You're playing hard to get, are you?'

He grinned and lunged at her once more, but this time she was prepared for it and, holding him at arm's length, she said coldly, 'I'm not playing at anything in particular, but I'm married to Gustav and you're married to Nicola, and don't you forget it.'

'I'm not likely to forget that I have a little wife waiting at home for me, but there's no harm in a little kiss, is there?'

'I don't wish to cause more unpleasantness than there already is at La Roche, but if you persist in this vein then I shall have to speak to Gustav about it.'

He released her then, but she did not like the look on his face when he said: 'I shall deny everything you say naturally. It will be your word against mine.'

'I don't somehow think he'll take yours, Russell, do you?' she remarked with unaccustomed mockery in her voice, but Russell seemed quite unperturbed.

'Honey, there's one other thing you should know about the man you married,' he smiled benignly, lighting a cigarette and leaning back against the door to observe her through narrowed eyes. 'Gustav has never had much faith in women, and I don't think even you have altered that.'

Caroline was not in a position to argue with him, and neither did she wish to. She knew Gustav well enough to know that Russell had spoken the truth, but not for anything in the world would she allow him to suspect how little influence she had over her husband.

'Take me back to La Roche, please,' she said coldly and, shrugging, he flicked his half-smoked cigarette out of the window and started the car.

That, Caroline hoped, was the end of that, but a few days later she was dismayed to discover that this was not so. While Gustav was taking a quick shower and changing into something more comfortable, Caroline went downstairs to join the others in the living-room where they usually met before going in to dinner.

The living-room was empty, or so it seemed, but she had barely stepped through the door when she found herself ensnared by a pair of strong arms.

'Got you this time,' Russell laughed down into her startled eyes. 'Now, how about that kiss you wouldn't give me the other day.'

'Russell, will you stop this at once!' she insisted fiercely, fighting him off with every bit of strength she possessed, but he appeared to possess a strength which could only be attributed to a man incensed.

'One kiss, that's all I'm asking,' he persisted hoarsely.

'No!' she cried anxiously, but his arms were too strong for her, and there seemed to be no way she could avoid that weak, seeking mouth.

His kiss filled her with revulsion, but, making use of the only weapon she possessed, she ceased her struggles and relaxed against him. Thinking, no doubt, that she was overcome with passion for him, he slackened his hold on her, and in that moment she thrust him from her and struck him a stinging blow across the cheeks.

'Ouch!' he shouted in surprise, his hand going to his face where the imprint of her hand was clearly visible against his pale cheek, but the next moment he lunged at her once more, and on this occasion his eyes were dark with anger. 'You little devil! I'll get you for that!'

'I wouldn't try that again if I were you, Russell,' a familiar voice intervened and, chilled to the marrow, Caroline swung round to face the door and the man who stood there observing them with a sardonic gleam in his catlike eyes.

'Gustav!' his name tripped anxiously off her lips, and although every part of her longed to fly into his arms, there was something in the set of his jaw that held her rooted to the spot.

Russell recovered himself with remarkable swiftness and, with an embarrassed little laugh that had a ring of falseness to it, he transferred the blame on to Caroline by saying, 'You certainly married a little tease, Gustav old man.'

A muscle jerked in Gustav's jaw, and for one frightening moment during those tense few seconds she thought that he was going to strike Russell, then a frozen smile curved his mouth as he stepped farther into the room to place a hard arm about Caroline's shoulders. There was no comfort in his touch, nor the slightest warmth in his eyes when he smiled down at her briefly before turning to Russell and saying,

'Did you think I didn't know that?'

Caroline knew a desperate longing to explain and, turning in the circle of his arm, she glanced up at him beseechingly. 'Gustav, I——'

'Later,' he cut short her attempt to tell him the truth, and moments later she knew the reason why.

Isobel and Nicola were walking into the living-room, and Caroline had to shelve her explanation for later that evening, but when she flashed a furious glance at Russell, she surprised a look of smug satisfaction on his thin face. He looked like a man who had succeeded in his objective, and suddenly she knew exactly who and what had prompted him to behave the way he had ... and why.

Misery, disgust, and fear were her companions for the rest of the evening. Nicola retired to bed soon after dinner, but Isobel and Russell remained a while longer in the hope of observing the results of their planned strategy, no doubt, but Gustav played the part of the attentive husband faultlessly as always.

Caroline's misery increased, and along with it her fear. She had only one piece of information with which to ward off his anger and his suspicions, but it was doubtful whether he would believe her, and his icy glance, when she finally found herself alone with him in the living-room, did nothing to bolster her courage.

'Gustav . . .' she began haltingly, rising from her chair to warm her chilled hands in front of the fire. 'About that incident you witnessed this evening . . .'

'What about it?' he prompted harshly when she faltered to a stop.

'Russell insinuated that I'd been encouraging him, but that's not true,' she continued, turning to glance imploringly at the man who stood smoking his cigar a slight distance from her, but there was no softening in his expression, and no sign of understanding as she added: 'I think I know why he has been behaving this way towards me lately.'

'I have no doubt that he finds you attractive,' Gustav drew his own mocking conclusions as he placed his cigar in a marble ashtray and dabbed with his handkerchief at the moisture in the corner of his mouth, then he turned to face her with a derisive smile twisting his lips. 'How do you feel about him, I'd like to know?'

'He's married,' she retorted in a shocked voice. 'And so am I.'

'Are you going to let that stop you from indulging in an affair with my stepbrother?'

Caroline went white, and it took a considerable effort to control the sick feeling at the pit of her stomach before she could trust herself to speak.

'Russell is a flamboyant rake,' she said at last. 'But I happen to like Nicola, and for that reason alone I haven't wanted to create a scene about his unwanted attentions.'

'That's was very nicely put, my darling,' he mocked her as he crossed the room to her side.

'Don't call me that!' she snapped, moving a pace away from him, and the disturbing allure his nearness had for her.

'I didn't notice you objecting to it before,' he taunted her.

'I couldn't very well object when I knew that it was for the benefit of Isobel and Russell, but at the moment there's no one here who needs to be impressed by such endearments,' she retorted, her eyes blazing up at him.

'Perhaps I should employ Russell's tactics in an effort to impress you,' he smiled down at her cynically and, moving with lightning speed, he caught her in his arms and held her a helpless prisoner against his broad chest.

'Let me go!' she cried furiously, fighting not only against the pressure his arms exerted, but against that despicable weakness that was invading her limbs as he buried his lips against her throat.

'I'll let you go when I'm good and ready, and not before,' he seemed to groan into her ear. 'Until then you will behave like my adoring wife and cease your flirtations with Russell, or I might——'

'Or you might what, Gustav?' she prompted angrily.

'I might just kill you!' he snarled with a viciousness that sent a chill of real fear racing through her veins.

'You'd be playing right into Isobel's hands if you did that,' she reminded him, too afraid to move for fear of her ribcage snapping beneath the pressure he was placing on it. 'Can't you see that this is what they want? Can't you see that Russell's disgusting flirtation with me was designed for the sole purpose of causing a rift between you and me in the hope that you'd find yourself without a wife on the given date?' She threw her head back to look a long way up into eyes which had lost a considerable amount of their coldness. 'I've discovered what they're aiming at. They want me out of the way, and I think they'll try anything to accomplish this.'

'Dammit, you're right!' he acknowledged grimly. 'With you out of the way I will only have fulfilled half the requirements to claim my inheritance.'

'Exactly,' she replied, breathing a little easier now that his arms had slackened their clasp about her. 'What are you going to do?'

'It's not what *I'm* going to do, but what *we're* going to do,' he answered in a clipped voice, glancing beyond her and back again to stare down into her wide, questioning eyes. 'We're going to let them see that they haven't succeeded, and we're going to start right this minute.'

Her lips were crushed beneath his before she could utter a sound, and when he finally gave her the opportunity to draw breath it was to seek out the sensitive, pulsating hollows against her throat.

'Gustav, please! I——'

'Shut up, you little idiot,' he growled in her ear. 'We're being observed from outside the window, so I'm determined to make this look good.'

Startled into submission by his disclosure, Caroline offered no protest when his lips found hers again, and despite the distressing thought that they were being observed, she found herself responding helplessly to his kisses. When Gustav lifted her in his arms and carried her from the living-room, she offered no resistance, but when he prolonged the demonstration after reaching the privacy of their bedroom, she thought it was time to make him aware of her unwillingness to be used in this manner.

'Gustav!' she gasped, dragging her lips from his. 'There's no one watching us now.'

'Who cares?' he laughed softly, lowering her on to the bed and undoing the tiny buttons of her blouse with a surprising deftness while his eyes seemed to burn their way right into her very soul. 'I'm just beginning to enjoy myself,' he added infuriatingly, and a low moan of pleasure escaped her when his sensual mouth began to explore the curve of her exposed breasts.

'I wish to heaven you'd leave me alone, Gustav!' she cried, but the husky note of passion was in her voice, and his soft laughter told her, humiliatingly, that he had heard it too.

CHAPTER NINE

CAROLINE was sunning herself out on the terrace one lazy Sunday morning while Isobel brewed up one of her usual storms in the kitchen. There was a touch of spring in the air even though that season had not officially started, but the sun was warm against her arms and legs as she lay back on the recliner watching the birds nesting in the trees, and she could not help thinking that, without Isobel and Russell, La Roche could truly be a paradise.

The wide brim of her sun-hat was pushed rudely over her eyes a few moments later and, swinging her legs to the ground, she pushed her hat on to the back of her head to find Russell grinning down at her. He had behaved himself since that time Gustav had found him trying to kiss her in the living-room and, despite herself, she found him pleasant company at times.

'For a man who's only been married a few short weeks Gustav leaves you alone rather a lot, doesn't he?' Russell remarked slyly, and this turned out to be one of those occasions when his insinuating remarks did nothing but anger her.

'Gustav has his business interests to take care of, and I don't intend to stand in his way,' she answered him coldly, rising to her feet and walking a little distance away to where the crimson bougainvillaea ranked profusely along one of the pillars.

'How very noble you sound,' Russell mocked her. 'I wish Nicola would allow me as much freedom to come and go as I please.'

'Don't you mean you wish your *mother* would allow you more freedom?' she asked bitingly, and when his glance darkened, she said: 'I don't think Nicola has been given much opportunity to make many demands on your time.'

'She's rather an insipid little creature at times, isn't she?'

'That's not a very nice thing to say about the woman you saw fit to marry, and who's going to have your child,' she said reprovingly, and Russell had the grace to lower his glance uncomfortably.

'I loved her when I married her,' he explained, 'but Mother has a way or organising everything. Including our marriage.'

'But why do you allow it?'

He pushed his hands into the pockets of his corded pants and shrugged. 'Mother has always done what she's considered was best for me.'

'Don't you think it's time you started deciding for yourself what's best for you and Nicola?' she asked sharply. 'Once the child is there, are you going to allow Isobel to usurp your authority as a parent?'

She did not expect an answer, and neither did he give one. Instead he said: 'I think I'll go for a walk in the garden.'

'If you take the path towards the fishpond you might find Nicola there,' Caroline suggested. 'I think she could do with a bit of cheering up.'

'Women!' he scowled back at her. 'You're all the same when it comes to ordering men about.'

'For once he's right,' a quiet voice spoke behind her, and her inward laughter stilled as she turned to confront Gustav who stood framed in the doorway with that familiar cigar clenched between his teeth. 'Women are all the same,' he continued in that lazy, mocking voice as he stepped out on to the terrace and strolled towards her, the muscles in his thighs straining against the material of his pants. 'They deceive you with a smile, and you're chained before you know it unless you're clever enough to escape in time,' he elaborated.

'Not all women are deceitful,' she argued, her senses stirring to the potent maleness of his tall, muscular body.

'I've lived by one golden rule for many years,' he reiterated, his eyes glittering cynically down into hers as he removed his cigar from his mouth. 'Never trust a woman. They lure you with their bodies and whisper lies in your ears, but if you're fool enough to fall for it you end up discovering that they were more interested in your bank balance than in you as a man.'

'That's a dreadful thing to say!'

'It's my belief that women will do anything for money.'

'Not all women, Gustav,' she protested, feeling a little sick inside.

'Don't exclude yourself, my dear wife,' he laughed harshly. 'It was your need for money that made it so easy for me to persuade you to marry me.'

She flinched visibly and lowered her eyes before the glowering intensity of his gaze. 'That's hitting below the belt!'

'It's the truth, nevertheless.'

'Yes, it's the truth,' she was forced to admit, 'but it's not quite the way you make it sound.'

He cupped her chin in his hand and raised her face to his, forcing her to meet the mockery and contempt in those peculiar eyes. 'Would you have married me if it hadn't been for the money?' he asked.

'Yes, she would have, the words sprang to mind. If

the circumstances had been different, and given time to
realise her feelings for him, she would have married him
even if he had not had two cents to rub together, but
she could never tell him that, she thought miserably as
she stared helplessly up into those compelling eyes which
were mocking her discomfort.

'Your silence confirms my statement,' he concluded
at last, releasing her chin with a cynical smile playing
about his mouth.

'Would you have married me if circumstances had
not demanded that you should produce a wife?' she
counter-questioned daringly.

'No, I wouldn't have,' he replied tersely and without
hesitation, cutting her to the quick with every word he
uttered. 'I would have taken you out a few times, and I
have no doubt that I would have seduced you eventually,
but the moment you began to bore me I would have
sent you a bouquet of flowers with my usual note saying,
"It's been fun, but this is goodbye".'

For a moment Caroline could not speak, then she
swallowed down the constriction in her throat and
breathed hoarsely, 'I think you're despicable!'

'Life's like that,' he observed callously. 'It's hello
today, and goodbye tomorrow, and there are seldom
any regrets that way.'

'I doubt if you've ever suffered the pangs of regret,'
she retorted, fighting back the waves of pain which threatened to engulf her. 'You haven't a heart, Gustav, only a
mechanised pump, and mechanical objects don't possess
the power to experience any of the finer emotions.'

'It doesn't pay to possess a heart where women are
concerned,' he replied cuttingly, his cold eyes narrowed
against the sun. 'By the time they're finished with you,
you don't even possess a soul you could call your own.'

To have continued this argument would have been like battering her head repeatedly against a solid wall like an idiotic ram, so she left him standing there on the terrace to seek the solitude of the spacious garden where the birds and the insects were the only ones to witness the tears spilling from her lashes on to her cheeks. There were still three weeks to go; three weeks of not knowing what to expect; of humiliations and insults, and a hopeless longing that lay heavy in her breast.

It should have come as no surprise to Caroline when Isobel confronted her at the breakfast table one morning with an offer that filled her with disgust.

'How much would it take for you to walk out, and stay out of Gustav's life?' Isobel came straight to the point. 'Name your price.'

Caroline was at first too shocked to speak, then she decided that she must have heard, or understood incorrectly, and finally she was forced to ask confusedly, 'Are you offering me money to leave Gustav?'

'That's exactly what I'm doing.' Cold, calculating eyes observed Caroline intently. 'How much?'

'Your offer doesn't interest me,' Caroline declined with a look of distaste mirrored on her face.

'Would five thousand rand make it sound more attractive?' Isobel persisted, and when Caroline did not reply she added with a smile, 'Think about it. Five thousand rand is a lot of money for a girl like yourself.'

'I don't need to think about it,' Caroline exclaimed angrily, pushing back her chair and getting up from the table. 'I won't be bribed into leaving Gustav, and I think your offer is deplorable!'

'Knowing Gustav, he won't be satisfied with you for long, then you will find that you will have to leave,'

Isobel replied with a slyness intended to tempt and, holding Caroline's angry glance, she added persuasively, 'If you leave now you'll at least be leaving with a sizeable amount of money in your pocket.'

Caroline recoiled inwardly from this woman, and with a coldness that bordered on intense dislike, she said: 'I don't want your money, Isobel. Not now. Not *ever!* If and when Gustav should wish me to leave, then I'll go the way I came in—with nothing in my purse.'

She walked blindly from the room without giving Isobel the opportunity to say anything further. In the hall she brushed past Nicola without really seeing her, and she almost took the stairs two at a time in her haste to reach the seclusion of her bedroom. Overcome by a wave of nausea, she sat down quickly on the edge of the bed, and the feeling departed slowly, leaving her face pale and damp with perspiration.

She had to talk to someone; she could not continue bottling things up in this way, but who could she trust with the knowledge she carried around with her? For endless seconds she stared at the telephone on the bedside table before her brain cleared sufficiently to think coherently, then she lifted the receiver and dialled a number with a hand that shook visibly.

'Margery Doyle, please,' she said when the switchboard operator's voice crackled in her ear.

Moments later, when Margery discovered the identity of her caller, she exclaimed delightedly, 'I was wondering when I'd hear from you.'

'Have lunch with me today, Margery?' Caroline asked without preamble.

'I'd love to,' her friend replied at once. 'Just tell me where.'

'What about the Crow's Nest?' Caroline suggested.

'It's the only decent restaurant close to the office that will give us plenty of time to chat before you have to rush off again.'

'My, but you're flying high, Caroline,' Margery teased goodnaturedly. 'The Crow's Nest is one of those posh and expensive places where executives treat their business associates to lunch.'

'While I still have wings to fly high, I might as well,' Caroline laughed with forced brightness, but her laughter did not, obviously, convince Margery.

'That sounds intriguing, I must say,' she replied with a note of curiosity in her voice and, afraid that someone might be listening in, Caroline ended the conversation abruptly.

'See you at one o'clock, then,' she said, and her suspicions were confirmed when she heard a decisive click on the line before her connection with Margery was severed.

Caroline replaced the receiver slowly and, closing her eyes, she fought back the second wave of nausea. Someone had listened in to their conversation. She could safely rule out Nicola as well as the servants, and that left only Russell and Isobel. Russell, usually late to rise, was still in his room, but there was a telephone extension beside his bed, just as there was one beside her own. Isobel, of course, was downstairs, and but a short distance from the telephone in the hall. Of the two she considered Isobel the most likely culprit, and she was made to realise once again how much care she would have to take in future. It was a sickening thought that not even her telephone calls were considered private, but what, she wondered, could one expect from a woman who had showed so little discretion by walking into a bedroom without knocking to surprise the occupants in an embarrassing state of undress? Never had Caroline imagined that anyone could be so vile, and she dreaded the thought of what Isobel might do next.

Deciding that it was best to stay out of everyone's way, Caroline remained in her room and had tea sent up to her instead of going downstairs to join the others. She sent a message down to the kitchen with Tilly to the effect that she would not be in to lunch, then she washed her hair, and selected a dark brown suit with its cream-coloured trimmings and blouse to match for her lunch appointment with Margery.

She shivered, almost as if she had left some evil force behind her when she drove away from La Roche later that morning and headed towards Epping. She had seldom left the house during the past weeks, except to buy a few necessary items, and not having to face Isobel and her son across the luncheon table was like escaping from the prison her life had become.

She arrived early at the Crow's Nest to secure a table which would give them sufficient privacy, and after telling the waiter that she would place their order later, she settled down to wait for Margery. She did not have long to wait, for Margery, her red hair bouncing about her face, entered the restaurant a few minutes later. She sent a quick glance across the interior with its white ceiling and polished wooden beams, then she made her way towards Caroline among the tables which were filling up quickly.

'Hm . . .' she smiled, giving Caroline the once over as she seated herself. 'I like your hairstyle, and I like your outfit. It looks expensive, and——' Her green glance sharpened as they fastened on to grey, shadowed eyes. 'Are you happy, Caroline?'

Taken aback, Caroline lowered her lashes. 'Yes, of

course. Why shouldn't I be?'

'You looked a little doubtful just then.'

'Oh, Margery ...' Caroline sighed, still doubtful about involving Margery in her personal problems. 'I would just like to talk to someone sane without being afraid I might say the wrong thing.'

'It's as bad as that, is it?'

Caroline looked up then into those green eyes observing her so intently, and after a poor attempt at smiling, she said thickly, 'It's bad enough.'

The waiter arrived to take their order, and while they waited their conversation skimmed the surface of many subjects. It was as if Margery sensed that it was not yet the right moment to prod her for further information, but when their plates were returned to the kitchen, leaving them to enjoy a cup of strong, aromatic coffee, Margery leaned towards Caroline with a purposeful look on her face.

'Is it the Lion?' she asked directly. 'Is he ill-treating you?'

'No, it's nothing like that. It's——' Caroline hesitated in her uncertainty, then she gestured helplessly with a slim hand. 'I really haven't the right to discuss anything so private and confidential, but I *must* talk to someone, and you're the only one I could think of.'

'You can trust me, my dear.'

'I know,' Caroline nodded soberly. 'That's why I'm here, and that's why I'm going to unburden myself to you.'

'I'm listening,' Margery announced with an encouraging smile, resting her elbows on the table in a comfortable listening attitude.

Caroline fought against her uncertainty for only a brief moment longer, then she started to speak. It came out haltingly at first, but her voice grew stronger as she went along. Margery listened without interruption, and it felt to Caroline as if she were shedding a great weight from her slim shoulders. Talking about it made the situation seem less frightening, and she found that she could almost laugh at some of the incidents she described to her friend. There was one thing, however, she could not discuss, and that was the existing situation between Gustav and herself. It was too private, too personal, and really concerned only themselves.

'I don't like the sound of the Lion's stepmother,' Margery observed when at last Caroline had lapsed into silence.

'She's desperate to get what she wants,' Caroline explained. 'That's why she went as far as offering me money to get out of the way, and I've become terrified at the thought of what she might do next.'

'You were a fool to have married Gustav in the first place.'

'I had no choice, if you remember,' Caroline whispered desperately. 'It was either him or Maxwell Hilton, and I think I would have killed myself rather than have had Hilton touch me.'

'You haven't fallen in love with Gustav, have you?' The question was aked with such an unexpected suddenness that Caroline had no time to conceal the truth in her eyes, and Margery, her keen glance missing nothing, groaned softly, 'Oh, my God, you *do* have a problem!'

'I couldn't help myself, Margery,' Caroline defended herself with a lump in her throat. 'I didn't want to love him. He's a hard, unfeeling brute most of the time, but——'

'But your tender heart melted in his expert hands,' Margery finished for her when she broke off abruptly and, clasping Caroline's hand across the table, she said decisively, 'Look, if I could give you any advice, then it's this. Stay out of their way as much as possible. If the house isn't big enough to accommodate you all without bumping into each other at frequent intervals, then I suggest you take a drive into town, or into the country. Have lunch somewhere, if you like, and don't return to the house until just before Gustav arrives home in the evenings.' Her fingers tightened about Caroline's as she added sincerely, 'If you should ever need me, then you know where I live. I have a spare bedroom, and I'll be only too glad to have your company.'

Caroline's heart warmed once again towards this woman who had become such a sincere friend in the short time they had known each other and, smiling shakily, she whispered, 'It's been a relief talking to you, Margery, and thank you.'

Caroline returned to La Roche afternoon in a much happier frame of mind, but a measure of fear returned when Isobel was the first person she encountered on her arrival, and with it came the tension that quivered through her as it did through an animal sensing danger.

'I would like to speak to you for a moment, Caroline,' she said, indicating that Caroline should precede her into the living-room.

Wariness stiffened Caroline's limbs, but when they were facing each other behind the closed door, Isobel surprised Caroline by saying, 'I owe you an apology. I had no right to offer you money the way I did this morning. One should know when to admit defeat, don't you agree?'

What new trick was this woman up to? Caroline wondered as she asked tritely, 'Have you admitted defeat, Isobel?'

'You're married to Gustav, aren't you?' Isobel smiled. 'And there's no way I can alter that.'

'I'm glad you feel this way about it,' Caroline murmured, not quite certain what to make of this new development. 'It will make life so much easier.'

'It certainly will, my dear,' Isobel smiled broadly, but her smile filled Caroline with suspicion.

If Isobel was genuinely sincere in the apology she had made, then Caroline would have nothing further to worry about, but what if this was not so? Was Isobel in earnest, or was she simply planning some new strategy in her attempt to outwit Gustav?

This question troubled Caroline considerably, but as the days passed, one after the other, in Isobel's seemingly congenial company, Caroline began to relax her guard. They were almost half way now into the first month of spring, and still Isobel maintained that charming front she had put up on the day she had apologised to Caroline. It was totally bewildering, but as the fifteenth of the month approached with agonising swiftness, Caroline found herself becoming more concerned with the realisation that her short stay at La Roche was coming to a swift and definite end.

Gustav, as yet, was showing no sign of growing tired of her. It appeared, in truth, as if his desire for her had increased, and caught in the passionate storm of his lovemaking, she constantly had to remind herself that it would not last. It was a despairing thought, knowing that she might soon find herself no longer wanted by the man at whose feet she had so foolishly laid her heart and her soul, and having to go into the future without him was something she thrust desperately to the farthest recesses of her mind. There was something else, too, that disturbed her of late. It was that feeling of nausea she had to cope with each morning when she had risen, but for the time being she considered it unimportant in the light of the unhappiness she would have to bear in the future.

On the day before Gustav could legally lay claim to his inheritance, Caroline went for a stroll after lunch, but when she came in out of the sun she found Nicola standing about on the terrace.

'Caroline, I must talk to you,' said Nicola, but the click of high heels in the hall behind her made her glance anxiously over her shoulder before she whispered with some urgency, 'Meet me at the fishpond in an hour.'

The words had barely left her lips when Isobel stepped out on to the terrace, and her sharp glance swerved at once in Nicola's direction.

'Isn't it time you went upstairs to rest?' she demanded of her daughter-in-law.

'Oh, yes,' Nicola said at once, casting a quick but imploring glance in Caroline's direction as she added in a strangely urgent voice, 'Caroline was just saying that she was on her way up as well.'

Caroline would have had to be dense if she did not realise that, for some obscure reason, Nicola did not wish her to be alone with Isobel. She wondered at the reason, but decided it would be best to wait until Nicola had had the opportunity to explain herself.

'I must admit that a rest before tea sounds inviting,' Isobel remarked, linking her arm through Nicola's. 'I'll come upstairs with you.'

The silence was oddly tense as the three of them trooped upstairs, and Caroline could not shake off the feeling that Isobel had appeared to be irritated by something. Was it perhaps the knowledge that she could do nothing to alter the course of events, or had her irritation merely been directed at Nicola for not adhering so strictly to the laws she had laid down for her?

Alone in her room Caroline's thought revolved around the peculiar incident on the terrace. Questions arose in her mind only to fade without answer, and as the travelling clock on the bedside cupboard ticked away the hour, she seated herself beside the window and relinquished the effort to fathom the extraordinary situation which had arisen.

There was peace at La Roche at this time of the day, and she envied Gustav his home as her glance swept over the spacious garden where signs of spring were clearly evident in the foliage of the trees and the colourful array of flowers. Without the disturbing presence of his step-family there could be tranquillity at La Roche, she realised yet again. Given the opportunity she would make it a haven for Gustav to return to at night after the pressures of the day, but he was a man unto himself. He enjoyed his freedom and his constantly changing choice of women with whom he whiled away his time when he was not at the office. He had made his own laws, and was bound by nothing, so what chance did she have of holding him once his interest had been sparked off in someone else's direction. Her days at La Roche were numbered; her position as his wife meaningless and dwindling into insignificance. She was his legal mistress, she thought distastefully, and she knew not to expect one iota of consideration more than he had shown any of the many women who had wandered in and out of his life in the past.

A flash of white in the garden below finally drew her attention and interrupted her distressing thoughts. It was Nicola, walking as quickly as she could in the direction of the fishpond, and casting several backward glances towards the house. Even from that distance Caroline could sense that Nicola was afraid, and the moment she disappeared among the trees, Caroline left her room and went downstairs as quietly as she could.

'Going for a walk, Caroline?'

'What?' Caroline swung round sharply to face the woman who had materialised, as if from nowhere, on the terrace, and making a desperate effort to regain her composure, she said with surprising calmness, 'Oh, yes ... yes, I am.'

'It's such a warm spring day,' Isobel observed, walking down the steps beside her. 'I think I'd like to go for a walk myself. I hope you don't mind if I accompany you, Caroline?'

'I don't mind at all,' Caroline lied helplessly, and with a touch of desperation.

Isobel waved her arm in the direction opposite to the one Nicola had taken. 'Shall we walk this way?'

Caroline nodded as amiably as she could, but her mouth felt dry, and her heartbeats had quickened with anxiety. *She knows,* she thought. *Isobel knows!* And all at once she knew that whatever it was that Nicola had wanted to say to her, it had been of vital importance. So important, in fact, that Isobel was doing her level best to prevent them from meeting.

Uneasy at the thought of Nicola waiting in vain for her to appear, Caroline attempted to give the impression that nothing was amiss, but a strange new tension was coiling through her despite her efforts to relax. She did not trust Isobel, she did not trust her for a moment, but Isobel seemed to be in a lighthearted, talkative mood, and her ramifications about La Roche, as it had been shortly after her marriage to Regardt de Leeuw, finally succeeded in quickening Caroline's interest and setting her at ease.

'This building was used once for the purpose of cooling the wine,' Isobel enlightened her as they approached an old building hidden partially behind the tall shrubs and trees. 'You'll notice the thick stone walls, and the absence of windows. It was designed, naturally, to keep out the air and the light,' Isobel continued, then she glanced at Caroline and asked casually, 'Does this sort of thing interest you?'

'Very much, yes,' Caroline admitted, her enthusiasm overriding her wariness.

'Shall we take a look inside?' Isobel queried, and without waiting for Caroline to reply she walked on ahead and lifted the heavy latch which had become rusted with age. 'It should still contain some of the relics from the past which you might find interesting and amusing,' she said over her shoulder as the solid oak door opened protestingly beneath her surprisingly strong hands.

She stepped inside ahead of Caroline and, unsuspectingly, Caroline followed her.

The smell of fermented wine and decay filled her nostrils, and when she reached Isobel's side she was no longer so sure that she wanted to explore further.

'It's rather dark, and it smells musty, doesn't it?' she remarked nervously as they moved further into the darkness.

'That's what comes from total disuse,' Isobel replied, unperturbed. 'There's a candle here somewhere . . . and matches, if I can find them.'

Caroline remained where she was while Isobel went in search of the candle and matches, but moments later her heart leapt into her throat when she heard the outer door slam shut.

'Isobel?' she asked anxiously, and still totally unaware of what had befallen her. 'I hope you find the matches quickly. It's become awfully dark now that the door has slammed shut.' There was no reply, and no sound of movement, only an eerie, dark silence. 'Isobel, are you there?' she cried out in a note of panic. *'Isobel!'*

With fear coursing through her veins, she stumbled over the cobbled floor as she felt her way back in the darkness along the short passage towards the door. Her hands reached out in feverish haste to find the latch, but there was nothing, only a short inefficient stub where it had at some time or another snapped off with age. Wild but recognisable laughter could be heard faintly beyond the door, and all at once Caroline knew the stark, terrifying truth. She was locked in; trapped in the old wine cellar, and Isobel was standing outside in the warm sunshine, laughing satanically at her easy victory.

'You can't do this to me, Isobel!' she cried hysterically, beating her fists against the thick wooden door. 'Let me out of here! *Please, Isobel, let me out!'*

The laughter grew fainter, but still Caroline continued to beat her fists against the heavy oak, pleading, begging, until her hands ached, and her throat felt raw with the effort.

It was hopeless; she knew it! She was trapped in this eerie darkness that reeked with the stench of age, and Isobel would make sure that she remained there until her diabolical plan had borne fruit.

CHAPTER TEN

NUMB with a mixture of cold and fear, Caroline sat down on the floor close to the door of the wine-cellar, and wrapped her arms about herself. There was no way of knowing how long she had been there, but it already seemed like hours. Rats, scurrying across the floor close to her, made her bite down hard on her lip in an effort not to scream out her horror. 'Dear God, please get me out of here,' she had prayed over and over, but there was nothing except the silent darkness, the stench, and the rats to contend with as the time dragged on. Tears were of no help either, and they had long since dried on her cheeks. The cold seemed to penetrate deep into her very bones, and a frozen feeling was moving steadily upwards from her fingers and toes.

In those long, dark, frightening hours she had had plenty of time to think, and clairvoyancy had not been needed to guess why Nicola had wanted to speak to her so urgently. 'Poor Nicola,' she thought, a hysterical little laugh bursting from her lips to echo weirdly into the empty corners of her prison. Nicola had wanted to warn her; to place her on her guard, but Isobel had been too clever for her daughter-in-law, and the trap had been sprung before Caroline had had time to sense the personal danger she was in.

Where was Gustav? she wondered frantically. Would he come searching for her, or would he think that she had chosen to desert him in the hour of his need?

'Oh, God,' she groaned out loud. 'Please let him find me. Please don't let me remain a prisoner here in this dreadful place throughout the long night and all of tomorrow until Isobel has succeeded in what she's set out to accomplish.'

A rat ventured too close this time and ran across her foot, and on this occasion she could not suppress the scream of terror that burst from her lips. She could not bear rats and mice. She could tolerate *anything*, but not those small, furry creatures, she thought hysterically, and as her imprisonment continued she found herself fighting against a terrible drowsiness in that airless building. Her head drooped until her chin came to rest on her breast, and it was with the greatest difficulty that she managed to keep awake, but some minutes later, or was it hours, a scraping sound wrenched her back to complete alertness.

There was someone on the other side of that door, and her suspicions were confirmed a second later when the door was flung open to admit the cool, but refreshing night air.

'Caroline?' a deep, familiar voice questioned sharply, and a flashlight was shone directly into her face, making her shut her eyes instinctively to ward off the stinging brightness. 'My God!' Gustav exclaimed, and he yanked her unceremoniously to her feet, literally dragging her outside.

Her release was as unexpected as her imprisonment had been, but from the midst of her intense relief there emerged a blinding fury which she found herself incapable of controlling. Being trapped for hours on end in that dark, damp wine-cellar seemed to have affected her normally rational mind, and the only thought that kept pounding through her brain was that Gustav was somehow to blame for the terrifying hours she had been forced to endure.

'Take your hands off me!' she almost screamed up at him, wrenching her arm from his clasp and stumbling beyond his reach on stiff, aching limbs. 'I've suffered nothing but insults, humiliation, and degradation since the day I came here to La Roche as your wife, and I refuse to endure it a moment longer. I'm leaving right this minute, and I don't jolly well care what happens to you, or your precious inheritance!'

'Pull yourself together at once!' he ordered sharply, looming above her like a dark, sinister shadow as he gripped her shoulders in punishing hands and shook her mercilessly until her teeth rattled. 'You'll see this thing through to the end. You owe it to me, and after that I couldn't care a *damn* what you do!'

'That's your biggest fault!' she cried chokingly, tears of helpless rage glittering in her eyes and making their way down her cheeks in the darkness. 'You don't care about anyone except yourself! You're an arrogant, self-opinionated, egotistical brute, and I *hate* you!'

'Shut up, you little idiot, and control yourself, or I might have to resort to slapping you hard!'

His voice had the effect of a whiplash, and her anger subsided, leaving her ashamed at the thought that, instead of being grateful that he had saved her from spending a night in that dreadful place, she had lashed out at him in a fury which should have been directed at Isobel.

'How—how did you know where to—to find me?' she asked finally, breaking the electrifying silence in a subdued, halting voice.

'Nicola told me about Isobel's plan to lock you up in here until after the lawyer had paid us a visit tomorrow,'

Gustav explained roughly, removing his jacket and placing it about her shaking shoulders. The warmth of his body still clung to the inside of the jacket, and she drew it about her more firmly with cold, trembling fingers while he continued his explanation. 'Isobel apparently filled a suitcase with some of your personal belongings, while Russell drove your car away and parked it somewhere safe to make your departure look authentic. It all sounds quite harmless now, but it wouldn't exactly have left a good impression with the lawyer tomorrow.'

'Yes, I know,' she managed through chattering teeth. 'It would have looked as if I'd run out on you.'

'If I didn't know you so well, and if Nicola hadn't made my task so much easier, they might have succeeded.' An odd little silence prevailed suddenly as they stood facing each other, then he placed a hard arm about her shoulders and said abruptly, 'Come on. I have plenty to discuss with my dear stepmother, and you might as well sit in on it.'

Caroline never quite knew how she managed to walk the distance back to the house, but she did so without complaint, and a great deal of trepidation at what she knew was to follow. This was to be a showdown; she could see that by the set of Gustav's jaw when he finally ushered her through the well-lit hall, and into the living-room where a silent threesome awaited their arrival with a mixture of expressions on their faces. Isobel wore a challenging mask that mirrored not the slightest sign of regret, while Russell sat with his hands dangling between his knees, and a sullen look on his lean face as he stared fixedly at the carpet beneath his feet. Of the three of them Caroline felt the most for Nicola. She looked pale and shaken, and very close to tears.

'I have a proposition to put to you, Isobel,' Gustav began after seeing to it that Caroline was comfortably seated in a chair close to the fire, and the hardness of his expression made her feel glad that his anger was not directed towards her at that moment. A tense silence prevailed while they waited for him to continue speaking, and when he did, two pairs of eyes in particular became riveted to his face. 'Sell me your shares in Protea Marine Engineering, and allow me to buy back my home,' he came straight to the point.

For a moment no one moved, then Isobel leapt out of her chair, reminding Caroline of a cat with its claws extended.

'You must think I'm mad!' she laughed again that satanic laugh Caroline had heard earlier that day.

'Not mad, Isobel,' Gustav corrected with a touch of that familiar arrogance. 'Just desperate for money.'

Her eyes narrowed calculatingly. 'Make me an offer.'

Gustav made her an offer which almost succeeded in taking Caroline's breath away. 'Take it or leave it,' he added harshly, 'but, whatever you do, I want you to get out of my life, and stay out.'

Gustav not only dominated the room at that moment, but everyone present, and Caroline, despite everything, was filled with admiration and a great deal of respect. He was the proud, arrogant master of La Roche, the dignified descendant of a long line of dignified forefathers, and he would not give up what was rightfully his without fighting for it to the bitter end.

'You'd be a fool not to take it, Mother,' Russell interrupted Caroline's train of thought.

'Shut up, Russell!' Isobel snapped, sending him a vicious glance that would have withered anyone other than her son.

'No, Mother, I will not shut up,' Russell announced adamantly, surprising them all and, rising to his feet, he looked his mother squarely in the eyes without so much as flinching. 'I no longer want to be a party to your devilish schemes. Either you take what Gustav is offering you, or Nicola and I will return to Namibia alone, and have nothing further to do with you.'

Isobel seemed to bristle with fury. 'How dare you speak to me like that!'

'I dare, Mother, because I'm tired of being the puppet while you pull the strings.' He held out his hand and drew Nicola to her feet to include her in what he had to say. 'Nicola and I want to live our own lives in future, and we want to make our own decisions without further interference from you.'

Isobel's dark eyes flashed venom at her daughter-in-law. 'I suppose you've put him up to this, Nicola!'

'Don't blame Nicola, Mother. Blame yourself,' Russell defended his wife, drawing her protectively into the circle of his arm. 'You overstepped the mark this time, and I'm ashamed to think that I was a part of it.'

'Have you quite finished?' Isobel spat out the words sarcastically.

'Yes, I've finished,' said Russell, drawing himself up to his full height, and addressing the woman who stood beside him with the light of pride shining in her eyes. 'Come along, darling,' he said. 'Let's go upstairs and pack.'

Caroline could not help but feel a certain amount of admiration for Russell. He had, at last, overcome the stumbling block of his mother's domination, and in the process he had become a man.

'Well, Isobel?' Gustav demanded, his voice slicing into Caroline's thoughts. 'Do you take my offer?'

'I'll take it, damn you, because I'm not prepared to live on the dividends only,' Isobel snapped furiously. 'And as far as La Roche is concerned, I shan't shed any tears at having to part with it, because you're thick-skinned enough to continue thinking of this as your home, and I'm damned if I want to end my days living under the same roof with you!'

'It's gratifying to know that you feel that way, Isobel,' he replied with biting sarcasm. 'I'll telephone my lawyer and instruct him to bring along the necessary documents when he calls on us tomorrow.'

Isobel did not wait to hear more and, after casting a crushing glance in her stepson's direction, she swept out of the living-room and slammed the door behind her with a force that rattled the windows in their frames. She was beaten, and ferocious in her defeat, but suddenly Caroline felt a deep compassion for her. She had fought, and she had lost, and Caroline felt sympathy for the loser. Her own father had been a loser, and soon, it seemed, she would be a loser herself.

'Well!' Gustav smiled derisively, rolling a cigar appreciatively between his fingers before he clipped off the end, and lit it. 'It seems as if it's going to be dinner for two this evening.'

The look of smug self-satisfaction that crossed his face made her wonder whether he would look like that on the day he sent her packing, and her insides recoiled instantly at the thought of food.

'If you don't mind,' she said coldly, shedding his jacket, 'I'm not hungry, and I'd rather go upstairs. I'm exhausted, and I need a bath.'

Gustav did not try to stop her. He merely bowed mockingly in her direction and, leaving his jacket on the chair she had vacated, she walked stiffly from the living-room to take the stairs slowly up to their bedroom.

After soaking herself in a hot, scented bath, she rubbed herself vigorously with a towel and slipped into her nightdress. She did not bother with her robe and slippers, and padded barefoot into the bedroom. She was tired; desperately tired, she told herself as she slid between the sheets, but it seemed she was not going to be given the opportunity to sleep just yet. The bedroom door was opened rather abruptly the next moment, and Gustav walked in carrying a tray that contained a plate of sandwiches and a glass of milk.

'You can't go to sleep on an empty stomach,' he said in that authoritative tone she loved, yet hated at times.

'You're very kind,' she said like a polite child, her body tense as she watched him place the tray on the bedside cupboard and seat himself beside her on the bed.

'Not kind,' he corrected, his eyes searchingly intent upon her pinched face. 'Concerned is the word. You've just suffered the nasty experience of being locked up in that old wine-cellar for several hours, and I feel partly to blame for it.'

Concern from Gustav was something quite alien. He had never shown her any concern in the past, so why should he do so now, and with a hint of sarcasm in her voice, she said: 'It was all in the line of duty, wasn't it? According to you any woman would walk through the fires of hell for seven thousand rand, or a similar amount, and that makes what I suffered something quite paltry, doesn't it?'

His jaw hardened, and his eyes became glacially cold as he rose to his feet to tower menacingly over her. 'I suggest you eat those sandwiches, and drink that milk before it gets cold. You're tired, and you don't know what you're saying.'

He turned on his heel and strode out of the room, and as she stared at the door he had closed so firmly behind him, Caroline felt the familiar sting of tears behind her heavy eyelids, but this was not the time for tears. There would be time enough for that later, she decided bitterly, and, blinking back the moisture, she reached for one of the sandwiches and bit into it.

She had not been hungry, but she was dismayed to discover that she had almost emptied the plate of sandwiches, and after drinking the warm milk thirstily, she switched off the light and lay back against the pillows. That hollow feeling at the pit of her stomach had gone, leaving her pleasantly tired, but as her eyelids drooped in the darkness she could not help wondering what the following day had in store for them all. Her thoughts were disjointed, however, and she promptly went to sleep.

Russell and Nicola were packed and ready to leave early the following morning, but Isobel had to wait to see the lawyer before she was ready to accompany them on their long journey back to Namibia.

It was an unusual day, with Gustav staying at home instead of going to the office. For the first time in weeks they all sat down to breakfast together, but an awkward silence hovered in the room, and no one seemed keen to break it.

The lawyer, a tall, wiry man in his fifties, arrived in time for tea that morning, and afterwards Gustav suggested that they retire to his study to sort out the business side of their affairs. Isobel, naturally, went with them, and that left Russell, Nicola, and Caroline with nothing to do but wait around until it was all over.

'I'm sorry about yesterday,' said Nicola when she found Caroline alone on the terrace just before lunch.

'When I heard what Isobel was planning I tried to warn you, but——'

'I know,' Caroline interrupted, shivering at the memory of the hours she had spent in that cold, dark cellar. 'I had plenty of time to think while I was trapped in that horrible place, and I realised then why you'd wanted to speak to me so urgently, but Isobel must have guessed what you were up to, for she caught me on my way out to meet you.'

'I waited for almost an hour,' Nicola whispered and, as the ready tears filled her eyes, Caroline leaned forward impulsively to kiss her on the cheek.

'Don't cry. It's all over, and I hope you're going to be very happy in future.'

'I will be. Oh, I *will* be,' Nicola replied enthusiastically, dabbing at her eyes with the handkerchief Caroline had unobtrusively placed in her hand, and Caroline could not help but envy her.

The lawyer did not stay to lunch, but he returned to La Roche shortly after two that afternoon with a batch of typed legal documents in his briefcase which needed to be signed. This did not take long, and within an hour the house was empty except for Caroline and Gustav.

As in everything else, Gustav had won, she thought that evening when they sat down to a silent meal. La Roche was his as it should have been from the start if Isobel had not used her diabolical influence to twist an old man's mind in his last moments on earth. The question that arose in her mind, however, was 'What happens to me now?' It was not something she wanted to think about, but she knew that, her purpose served, she would soon be found redundant.

She was standing in front of their bedroom window later that evening, staring down into the moonlit garden below, when Gustav emerged from the dressing-room and crossed the length of the room to join her there.

'You haven't said much this evening,' he said, his masculine cologne enveloping her and stirring her senses. 'Come to think of it, you haven't said much all day.'

She turned to face him then, her grey eyes veiled as they met his intense scrutiny. 'All I can think of saying at the moment is "congratulations", and all I can ask is 'what happens next?" '

'We go on as we are,' he replied enigmatically.

'For how long?'

'For as long as I still want you,' he replied with infuriating casualness.

'Surely I have some say in this matter?' she demanded, her eyes sparkling with anger. 'Or do you consider that having bought me you have sole right to discard me only when it pleases you?'

'I would call what extra time we have together a bonus, wouldn't you?' he questioned mockingly, his hands sliding possessively over her hips and drawing her relentlessly closer to him.

'Don't touch me!' she cried in anger, fighting him off, but her strength was no match for his, and she found herself trapped against the hard length of his body.

'I'll touch you, and make love to you, whenever I please,' he stated with calm, infuriating arrogance. 'You're mine for as long as I care to have you, and you'd better accept it that way.'

She renewed her struggles with more vigour and, beating her fists against his chest, she hissed, 'You can't treat me this way and think you can get away with it!'

'I'll treat you any way I please, you little wildcat,' he laughed mockingly against her lips as he pinned her arms helplessly at her sides. 'And you'll stay with me for as long as it pleases me, because that's what you want, and don't deny it.'

She could not deny it, not even if she had wanted to, for his mouth was devouring hers, and her body was melting against his with a hunger and yearning which she knew would never be totally satisfied.

The following day, alone at La Roche, Caroline had plenty of time to think. She could not remain a day longer, for the uncertainty would drive her insane, and above all she would not be able to bear the humiliation of Gustav coming home one evening to tell her that he no longer wanted her. She was going to have his child, she knew this now, and he most certainly would no longer want her in his home once he discovered this.

She finally decided that she would save Gustav the trouble of throwing her out by leaving La Roche that same afternoon. He had humiliated her enough in the past, and she was determined not to be humiliated again.

It was not an easy decision to make; to walk out on the only man she would ever love, but pride dictated that she could not continue living with him under these circumstances. She refused to be his plaything; a toy he could discard when it suited him, and that left her with only one thing to do. She had to go away, and there was only one person she could go to at such short notice.

It was long after five that afternoon when Caroline parked her small Austin in the parking lot behind a modern block of flats in the city. She carried her suitcase wearily into the building, and took the lift up to the third floor. Having made her decision, she had packed in a hurry for fear of the possibility that she might change her mind, and taking her future into her own hands had left her feeling exhausted and drained of emotion.

'Caroline!' Margery exclaimed when she opened her door seconds after Caroline had rung the bell and, grasping the situation at once, she removed the suitcase from Caroline's numb fingers. 'Come inside,' she ordered quietly.

'Forgive me for arriving so unexpectedly, but——'

'Here . . . sit down before you fall down,' Margery instructed, drawing Caroline towards a chair and waiting until she was seated before she asked, 'What happened?'

'It's all over,' Caroline explained dully.

'Did he tell you to go?'

'No, but——' Caroline gestured tiredly with her hands, 'I just couldn't go on living with him not knowing when he might decide to throw me out. He's always made it perfectly clear that our marriage would last only as long as it suited him, and I—I just couldn't face the humiliation of—of being told to go.'

Her control snapped at that point and, burying her face in her hands, she burst into tears. Not since her father's death had she wept such long and bitter tears, and Margery left her to cry until she leaned against the backrest of the chair, drained and lifeless.

'Drink this,' Margery ordered, placing a lethal-looking drink in her hand. 'It will do you good.'

The liquid scalded her throat, and burned its way down into her stomach. She grimaced at the revolting taste, but Margery insisted that she drink it all, and soon she began to feel the soothing effect of it. A warmth began to spread throughout her entire body, and her taut muscles relaxed gradually.

'You're very kind, Margery,' she smiled faintly, wiping away the final traces of her tears. 'There was just nowhere else I could go.'

Margery squeezed her arm lightly. 'You did the right thing coming here to me. I'll look after you.'

The rest of the evening was something of a blur to Caroline. Margery prepared a meal for them, and Caroline went to bed soon afterwards to sleep through the night as if she had been given a sedative.

She barely touched her breakfast the following morning, and settled instead for a cup of coffee. It was impossible to shake off the enormity of what she had done, or to ignore the emptiness of the future which she now had to face. She had made the right decision, instead of having Gustav make it for her some time in the future, and she would have to bear the cost of it for the rest of her life. Gustav belonged in her past, and she would have to make sure that he remained there.

'You love him very much, don't you?' Margery observed quietly and shrewdly as they faced each other across the table in the small kitchen, and the hot tears that filled Caroline's eyes confirmed her statement. 'Have you tried telling him?' Margery asked.

Caroline made an effort to pull herself together, but she could not quite control the tremor in her voice. 'How do you tell a man with a heart of stone that you love him? He mocks the very word, and I would end up being humiliated. There's one other very important reason why I couldn't stay with him; not even if he asked me.' She bit down hard on her quivering lip and, meeting Margery's questioning glance, she said unsteadily, 'I'm going to have a child.'

Margery's eyes widened in dismay. 'But, my dear——'

'He dislikes children, you see,' Caroline interrupted bitterly. 'He told me so himself.'

For the first time since knowing Margery, Caroline

saw her at a loss for words, then she picked up her handbag and walked round the table to Caroline's side.

'Look,' she said firmly, placing a comforting arm about Caroline's shoulders. 'Make yourself at home, and take things easy. Who knows, in a few days the situation might have sorted itself out into its proper perspective.'

Margery had almost reached the kitchen door when Caroline thought of something, and she called out her friend's name anxiously. 'You won't tell him where I am, will you?'

'I won't tell him,' Margery promised solemnly, and a few moments later Caroline found herself alone in her friend's spacious flat.

To keep herself occupied, Caroline washed the dishes and tidied the place, but by ten o'clock that morning she found herself with nothing more to do, and it was then that the agonising thoughts returned to torture her.

'Dear God,' she prayed silently, her thoughts leaping back to that wet, wintry night they had met, 'put a light in the window for me. I'm lost.'

Minutes later the doorbell rang and, thinking that it was a salesman taking a chance on someone being home, she went to answer it, but her face paled and her heart almost leapt out of her breast when she found Gustav standing on the doorstep.

She should have known that this would be one of the first places he would look for her, she told herself angrily, but a tenderness invaded her heart when she took a closer look at him. He was shaved and immaculately dressed as always in a dark, businesslike suit, but he bore the look of a man who had not slept all night. His eyes were heavy-lidded, and his expression was grim, but this was no time to feel sorry for him, she decided, pulling herself together with an effort.

'What do you want?' she asked sharply when she managed to find her voice.

'To talk to you,' he answered abruptly, stepping across the threshold and closing the door behind him.

Her emotions were in a frantic turmoil at the sight of him, but she was determined not to let him see the effect his disturbing presence was having on her.

'I don't think I have anything to say to you except goodbye,' she said coldly, 'and now that I've said it, you can get out of here.'

'Don't speak to me like that!' he seemed to grind out the words. 'I shan't tolerate it!'

'I don't think you're still in a position to dictate to me,' she contradicted, turning away from his potent maleness to enter Margery's lounge. 'I've done all that was required of me. Isobel has a fat banking account—and you have your home and Protea Marine Engineering under your wing, so to speak. All that remains now is for us to obtain a quiet and, I hope, quick divorce to bring our distasteful association to an end.'

Strong hands, so achingly familiar, gripped her shoulders and turned her relentlessly to face him, but she could not meet those compelling eyes when he asked, 'Can you honestly say that every facet of our marriage has been distasteful to you?'

'I don't want to discuss it. Not with *you*! Not with *anyone*!' she retorted angrily, trying to free herself, but his hands merely tightened on her shoulders.

'You sound as if you're ashamed of what happened,' he remarked softly, his tawny glance intent upon her downcast eyes, her pale cheeks, and the generous, quivering softness of her mouth.

'I *am* ashamed!' she admitted fiercely. 'I'm ashamed that the need for money forced me to agree to marry you, and I'm ashamed of what you made me do to get you what you wanted.' Her eyes rose and fell before his once more, then, throwing caution to the wind, she confessed in an agonised voice, 'But most of all I'm ashamed to think that I once thought I loved you.'

'Caroline . . .' he began, his voice sounding strange, but she broke free of him and crossed the room to stand staring out of the window with unseeing eyes.

'You don't deserve to be loved; you deserve to be despised,' she said jerkily over her shoulder. 'You don't need love, and neither can you give it. Like the name of your home, you have a rock where your heart ought to be, and all I can feel for you is pity.'

'I don't need your pity, Caroline,' he said thickly, coming up behind her. 'I need *you*.'

'For what purpose this time?' she demanded sarcastically, finding the courage to swing round and face him. 'Is there some goal you haven't yet achieved in life which needs the acquisition of a wife?'

'I credited you with more understanding, Caroline,' Gustav replied tiredly but admonishingly. 'Don't you realise how difficult I'm finding it to give you my reasons for coming here to see you?'

She stared up at him now, loving him and hating him simultaneously, but also determined not to give in to his demands on this occasion. 'Why did you come, Gustav? To gloat? To humiliate me for the last time before you go your merry way?'

An unfathomable expression flitted across his face, then his features hardened. 'Your place is at La Roche, and I've come to take you back with me.'

'Really?' she laughed mockingly. 'And do you think

you merely have to snap your fingers for me to come running eagerly back to you?'

'For God's sake, Caroline! Do you want me on my knees at your feet?' he demanded hoarsely, and everything stilled within her when she noticed the tortured, agonised expression on his rugged face.

Suddenly there was nothing she wanted more at that moment than to fling herself against his rock-like body, and to feel his arms tighten about her, but she dared not. She could not risk being held for a while, and finally rejected. Gustav had wanted other women before her; some perhaps for longer periods than others, and there was no reason to think that she would not go the same way they went.

'I don't think I would like to see a man with your pride and dignity lowering himself to such an extent,' she managed at last in a lifeless voice.

'What do you want, then?'

'I want you to go away. I want you to leave me in peace, because I can't stand this a moment longer,' she almost pleaded with him now, and he went strangely white about the mouth during the ensuing silence.

'I'll go, Caroline, but before I do there are a few things I must say,' he insisted at length, taking her by the shoulders once more as he forced her to meet his eyes, and what she saw there melted that icy feeling about her heart to send a strange glowing warmth through her veins. 'If there's anything worth having in my life, then that something is you,' he explained, his voice deepening, and vibrant with emotion. 'You once said you would feel sorry for me when I found that I couldn't buy love like everything else. Feel sorry for me now, Caroline. I can't buy what little love you may still have left for me, but I know that a future without you will not be worth living. I can't bring myself, yet, to say the words you might want to hear. They might sound false, coming from me, but perhaps you'll understand if I say that I would gladly give up everything I possess just to have you.'

The shutters were down, and his naked soul was there for her to see in his eyes, but, as the most incredible joy swept through her, she felt compelled to say, 'I can't go back to you. Not now.'

His hands fell away from her, and his haggard expression was almost too much for her to bear. 'Do you have no feeling left for me?'

'It's not that,' she shook her head miserably. 'Do you remember telling me once that you wouldn't be able to tolerate a screaming brat in your home?'

He looked startled for a moment, then his expression softened incredibly, and his hands came up to frame her face with a gentleness that was touching.

'My darling,' he murmured. 'If you're trying to tell me that you're pregnant, then I can't think of anything that would please me more than for you to have my child.'

Her bewildered eyes stared up into his. 'But you said——'

'I said a great many foolish things at one time that have no bearing on the way I feel now,' he interrupted, the smile in his eyes finally softening his hard features.

'Dare I believe you?' she whispered brokenly.

'Come home with me, my darling.' He brushed the tears from her cheeks with warm, caressing lips. 'Pack your things, and leave a note for Margery.'

'But what will I say?' she asked unsteadily, confused and deliriously happy at the same time.

'Tell her that your husband needs you, and that he

wants to spend the rest of his life making up for all the unhappiness he may have caused you when he was still fool enough to think that no woman would ever succeed in squeezing blood out of the rock he possessed for a heart,' he told her with a touch of the old mockery gleaming in his catlike eyes, but there was tenderness there too, and love, and it touched her heart as nothing else could.

'Oh, Gustav!' she sighed, melting against him contentedly, and he wasted no time in moulding her to him, and kissing her as she had never been kissed before. There was the passion she knew so well, but there was also an underlying gentleness, and she responded deliriously until their hunger for each other made them draw apart a little breathlessly. Her fingers caressed the rugged contours of his face in a way she had never dared to do before, and the eyes she raised to his no longer hid the feelings she had been forced to veil for so long. 'I've been so miserable loving you, and thinking you could never care for me in return.'

'You foolish child,' he laughed softly, a warmth in his eyes that she had never seen there before, but it was meant only for her, she knew that, and it had the power to stir her emotions. 'No matter how much I've fought against it, you've been the light of my life from that night I dragged you out of the rain and into my cottage,' he murmured, capturing her hand in his and burying his warm, sensual mouth against her pulsating wrist. 'I was enchanted with you, and before we parted company I knew that I wanted you more than I'd ever wanted any woman before. I saw in you, too, the solution to my problem, and I couldn't have been more relieved when I discovered that your engagement to Dennis what's-his-name was something of the past. I thought it would be the easiest thing on earth letting you go once you'd served your purpose, but right from the start I found myself fighting like the very devil against feelings that were becoming too strong for me to cope with.'

'I love you, Gustav,' Caroline whispered, unable to suppress the words that seemed to burst from her over full heart, and he groaned as he dragged her up against him, his seeking mouth exploring every part of her delicate features before capturing her quivering, eager lips.

In time, perhaps, he would learn to tell her of his love for her, but at that moment words were unnecessary. The Lion of La Roche had chosen her because he loved her; it was there in his eyes, his lips, and his touch, and she could think of nothing she wanted more than to have the privilege of sharing his life, and having his child.

Harlequin Plus

A WORD ABOUT THE AUTHOR

Yvonne Whittal's childhood was spent in Port Elizabeth, on the southern tip of Africa. She recalls dreaming of the day she would be able to travel to unknown countries.

At a very early age she began scribbling stories. Her ambition to be a writer resurfaced after her marriage and the birth of three daughters. She enrolled in a writing course, began submitting short stories to publishers and, with each rejection letter, became all the more determined.

Turning to the task of writing a full-length book, Yvonne was encouraged by a young woman with whom she was working—an avid reader of romance fiction and a helpful critic.

For Yvonne Whittal, there is no greater satisfaction than writing. "The characters become part of my life," she says, "and when I come to the end of each novel, realizing that I now have to part with my manuscript, it is like saying farewell to dear and trusted friends."